I0531582

WHILE REBELS SLEEP

By

Mila A. Ballentine

ISBN: 978-0-9794172-52

CHAPTER ONE

On the first day of school, Mr. Duncan made a point to tell them he was forty. He had gone gray by thirty-five but it worked for his profession. Besides teaching at Yellow Springs High School, he also taught an Advanced Poetry course at a community college. According to him, gray hair made him look more distinguished. He joked that 'dealing with high school students had a way of sucking the melanin out of teacher's hair.' The morning rays pierced through the window, and his hair glistened when the clouds released the sun. Mr. Duncan had a habit of pacing from one end of the blackboard to the next. He was so tall his head nearly reached the top of the blackboard. It was hard not to notice his smooth tanned skin against his deep-blue eyes. The salt and pepper beard that sprouted from his masculine jaw line only added to his charm. Clearly, he was once a handsome young man with black hair. He stood still. A gray wool blazer draped his broad shoulders over a light-blue formal shirt. A red handkerchief peeped out of the breast pocket of the blazer, and if he wasn't wearing khaki pants and brown loafers, something was terribly wrong.

Mr. Duncan's students didn't care about his hair. All they cared about was that he made the forty-five minutes in his class interesting. When he sensed his students were bored, Mr. Duncan shared stories about the places he'd traveled and books he had published. He often assigned weird prompts for the class to base their poems on. When they were finished, the students awkwardly read their poems to the class. Everyone came up with different poems, and all of them were equally unique.

Sometimes no matter how interesting his class was Anya managed to fall asleep. Mr. Duncan rambled on to the class about the day's lesson.

"Anya, can you explain the difference between a stanza and prose?" Anya's head nodded and her eyes opened. Her long auburn hair laid like rippled silk on the desk.

"Kibbles and bits," she mumbled and rested her head on the desk. The class erupted in laughter. Mr. Duncan cleared his throat.

"Prose has no rhythm or line structure, whereas, stanzas have four or more lines or a rhyme scheme. If you were paying attention, Miss Polanski, you would know that."

The bell rang. Anya sluggishly got out of the chair.

"Wait a minute, Miss Polanski. I'd like to have a word with you." She dragged her feet as she walked over. Mr. Duncan sat at the edge of his desk and waited for her to finish the walk of shame. She primed herself for a tongue-lashing. Her mouth appeared to pout but her lips were naturally plump.

"What's going on with you? You've been falling asleep in my class a lot lately."

"I'm sorry. It won't happen again. I promise." She walked out of the classroom and went to her next class.

The school day couldn't go by fast enough. Anya daydreamed through the next few classes except for orchestra. She had no choice. Charles walked into the classroom. He had a new military-style haircut and his blonde hair and pale complexion made him appear bald. Charles always wore shirts smaller than his actual size. Anya tried not to look, but it was hard not to. His nipples were like giant apostrophes. In the summer, his look drew attention to his physique. In the winter, it was a different story. His nipples visually pierced the fabric. It drew attention from the girls and encouraged a giggle or two. One boy in particular was vocal about his feelings on the matter. It was hot outside, so the air conditioning was on inside. Bradley glared at Charles. "Dude, you should borrow your sister's bra."

"Shut up Bradley! Go suck an egg!"

Bradley got out of his seat. He had a six-inch advantage over Charles. His overly gelled and starched black hair made it easy to spot him in class. In-between songs, Ms. Wick allowed him to contort his body into creepy poses to entertain the class. And by the looks of it, he was about to entertain them in a different way.

Charles and Bradley started smacking each other in the head while the other students chanted "cuff, cuff, cuff." The smacks turned into punches in the arm and gut. All while the two boys laughed it off. Then they started kicking each other in the shins. They fell to the floor and tumbled down the layered floor like tumbleweed.

Ms. Wick had a cute dainty face, and long black curly hair, but she also had a bad case of elephantiasis in one of her legs. Her school attire consisted of spaghetti strap shirts, cardigans paired with long flowing skirts and Velcro snap sandals, even in the winter. When she left the room there was always someone stationed at the door. When the lookout saw her, he would say, "Big foot is coming!" but that didn't happen this time. The lookout was busy watching the fight.

Ms. Wick walked in the room and slammed her books on the desk. "Stop it. Now!" She tried to pull them apart and got tossed to the side. Anya and her best friend, Brittney Spindle, helped Mrs. Wick to her feet. Mr. Beans heard the commotion from next door and came rushing in. He stood six feet three inches tall, and wore coke-bottle glasses. His pants looked like they were terrified to touch his ankles and were so tight that his nuts and bolts were on display. Rumor had it that he had the 'hots' for Ms. Wick. He started working out to impress her, and by the looks of it his hard work paid off. He pulled Charles and Bradley apart like a referee. The students called him Mr. Beans but his real name was Mr. Briggs.   Mr. Briggs held their shirts in the grip of his fists, slightly raising them, exposing their belly buttons.

"Be cool," he said. Charles put his hands up while Bradley hung loose like a scared chump.

"I'm cool. Were cool," Charles, responded.

"Let's take a walk to the principal's office." Mr. Briggs loosened his grip on their shirts and pointed in their faces in a sweeping motion.

"No funny business. You hear me?"

Not a word came out of their mouths. Mr. Briggs and the two boys walked out of the classroom and down the corridor.

"Okay class, get back to work. I want you to practice *Advent Rising*," Ms. Wick said. The room filled with the sound of violins, cello, bass and violas. They played as if nothing ever happened. *Normal? Yes. Bizarre? No!*

Anya managed to avoid the attention of the masses of students by hanging out in the most undesirable locations, study hall and the library. Nerds rarely caused trouble unless you tried to give them wedgies. Study hall was a place to complete homework so students could do whatever they wanted to do after school. In the library, she could avoid the emos and Goth's. The jocks were too busy flexing their pecks and collecting digits in the highly populated hallways and courtyard.

Todd was the exception to the rule. He transcended the other groups; his dad was a member of one of the most powerful political families in Yellow Springs, the Brent's. He made her blood curl. Anya hated him ever since he turned Mindy, an outgoing paraplegic, down when she asked him to the dance last year. The bell rang and students lined up outside to get on the bus. Anya walked through a side exit and past a group of students. Hundreds of students waited outside for the buses that took up the entire length of the block. She walked to the front of the school and waited for her dad. Todd walked toward her and sat on one of the short, flat-top concrete poles that bordered the main office building.

"Hi."

Anya looked next to her, "Oh hi." She took her IPod out of her jacket, turned it on, and inserted the headphones.

"I was wondering if you'd go to the dance with me." She looked in the opposite direction.

"Anya—."

Her father pulled up in his 1969 Chevrolet Camaro SS.

"Hi, Mr. Polanski."

"Hey Todd," he extended his hand and gave Todd a loose handshake. How are you doing?"

"I'm good. Just looking out for your daughter."

"Good," Alan replied.

Anya picked up her bag, entered the car, and slammed the door.

"Hey! Easy on the ride," he said in a firm tone.

"Please drive. Ugh, I hate him." She growled her words. Alan pulled away from the curb and drove out of the school parking lot. He banked the corner and entered Enon Road.

"Well, he sure seems to like you." Alan looked at Anya.

"Eww. Never," she crunched her face in disgust. Alan parked in front of the bookstore.

"I have to work late. You'll have to take the bus home."

"Okay," she kissed him on the cheek and left the car. He waited for a moment. A light drizzle began to fall. Anya ran underneath the awning in front of the door and entered the store.

"Good afternoon, Mrs. Berry."

"Hello, we have a lot to get done today. A shipment came in and I'd like to get it all done by closing time."

"Okie dokie."

Anya opened the box with a box cutter, placed rows of books on the counter and started entering the bar codes into the computer system. Luckily, it was a slow day so she was able to concentrate on completing the task. Mrs. Berry wasn't able to help. She was busy helping customers who took up far too much time without purchasing anything.

The telephone rang, "Hello, Rare Finds Bookstore. How can I help you? Ah ha, *The Pickle in the Pod*. One second while I check our database." She typed in the entry. *Not found was the message that came up.*

"I'm sorry, but we don't have that title, but we can place an order for you." She jotted down the name and number on an index card and placed it between the keyboard and the monitor.

"Mrs. Berry, I'm finished entering all of the books. Would it be okay if I left early?"

"Sure, I'm about to get out of here anyway. I'll be right back. I just have to take this to the office. She went into the back office, put the cash in the safe, and dimmed the lights.

"All right, let's go." Mrs. Berry put her purse over her shoulder.
They left the store and stood under the awning while Mrs. Berry locked the door. It was raining and the flow continued to increase.

"Is your dad picking you up?" She looked at the heavy rain pouring off the sides of the awning.

"No, I'm taking the bus."

"Are you sure? I don't mind taking you."

"Thanks for offering, but I'll take the bus." "Okay. I'll see you tomorrow then." Mrs. Berry opened her umbrella and walked over to her car that was parked a few steps away. She fiddled with the keys as she tried to open the door. Mrs. Berry entered closing the door almost all the way but her hand still held the umbrella over the door. She closed the umbrella, pulled it inside quickly and closed the door. Anya looked both ways, pulled her jacket over her head, and sprinted across the street to the sheltered bus stop.

Mrs. Berry's high beam shined brightly from the other side of the street and the windshield wipers were on overdrive. Anya waved; Mrs. Berry honked the horn and drove away. While Anya waited for the bus, there was a split second where she wished she'd taken Mrs. Berry up on her offer. Then she remembered the time she got a ride with her last winter. The roads were untreated, filled with two inches of ice, and three inches of compacted snow. Mrs. Berry hit an ice patch above the snow and turned the steering wheel sending the car into a 360-degree spin. They narrowly missed a light pole.

Anya came dangerously close to peeing her pants. Since then the Nile could roll through Yellow Springs, and if Mrs. Berry were the only one with a canoe, she'd rather climb on top of a roof and wait for help. A squirrel could run out in the road in front of her car and she would drive into a tree instead of stepping on the brakes.

Anya stood there half-drenched waiting for the bus, when a young man dressed in black ran to the bus stop, and stood under the shelter. He was completely soaked and flipped his hair away from his face. Beads of water flew in the air and landed on the side of Anya's face.

"Hey." She snarled.

"Sorry," he said.

The bus pulled up and sent a wave of water flowing on the sidewalk. She put the jacket over her head and entered the bus. The young man entered behind her, walked past rows of empty seats to the back of the bus, and sat down. She sat in the seat directly behind the Plexiglas frame of the driver seat. Anya tried not to look at him, but it was hard not to notice someone wearing all black and combat boots. Perhaps he escaped from one of those places where parents send their unruly kids, or maybe he played in a heavy metal band. Who knows, he probably squashed bugs for a living with those heavy boots. A soft giggle escaped her lips. He looked at her. She turned her head and looked out the window.

He pulled the yellow cord to request a stop. There was zero visibility. He ran into a sheet of heavy rain. The windows were misty, so Anya used her hand to wipe away the moisture. She saw him run for shelter inside a doorway of a corner store. By now, her dad was worried and called her. She answered the phone.

"Hi, dad."

"Where are you?"

"I'm close, but a tortoise could get home quicker than I could. I'm just glad I'm not driving because it's hard to see past the windshield."

"Okay, I'll see you soon."

Her stop was up ahead, so she pulled the yellow cord to request a stop. Anya got off to see her dad waiting under the bus shelter. He opened the umbrella and she dashed from the bus to get under it. They huddled close to each other and walked home.

CHAPTER TWO

Anya stared at her reflection in the mirror. She touched the birthmark below her left breast and hissed at her reflection. She walked through the hallway and into the living room.

"Dad, can you give me a ride to work?" Alan sat on the couch flipping through channels.

"Sure, Pumpkin." He turned off the TV.

"I hate it when you call me Pumpkin." Anya went out the front door and Alan followed.

"I know but I can't help it. Let's go." Alan grabbed his keys from the counter and went out the door. She sat on the leather seat and the searing heat burned her skin.

"OMG dad, it's like 90 degrees out here. You should park the car in the garage." She sat with her arms folded.

"In the winter, the seat is cold and in the summertime hot."

Alan glared at his daughter, "watch your tone." He lowered the zipper on his sweater. No matter the temperature, he wore a plaid shirt beneath a utility zip sweaters and jeans. His favorite saying was, 'if you don't like the weather, wait five minutes and it will change.' Last year, they experienced three seasons in a day.

"You can buy one of those cars with seat warmers."

"I like my vintage car just fine, thank you."

"So how is work going?"

Anya put on her headphones and rest her head back on the headrest. The buildings blurred as he drove down the road, temporarily teleporting her to Nottingham, an invented place in her mind where she would go occasionally. In Nottingham, nothing was relevant but her existence and oxygen. She was the sole citizen of a lost clan that trekked across time to camp out in--of all places--Yellow Springs, Ohio. In the midst of the serene city, she stood on a cliff. A black cape covered her long Auburn hair. She methodically waved the staff, igniting change as her green eyes reflected flames that engulfed the city. A loud thump cut through the sound of the wind. The passenger-side front wheel entered a pothole.

"Oops, sorry, missed that one," Alan said.

"You didn't miss it." Anya's looked at her father and she smiled. He looked younger than his age and in the past had been mistaken for her brother. He remedied the confusion by growing a beard. His beard was a tad bit lighter than his short dark-brown hair. Now Anya had to live with a hairy mammoth. No matter how long he stayed in the sun, he was pale.

Alan sensed her staring at him. "What?"

"Love you Dad."

"Love you too, Pum—."

"Don't even say it."

He chuckled, "sorry."

Anya sprayed Windex on the inside of the Rare Finds Bookstore front glass window. A shirtless young man walked by and stopped. He flexed his muscles and made his pectoral muscles twitch.

"Pervert." She put down the towel, went to the back of the store and stocked the shelves.

Brittany Spindle coasted down the sidewalk with Heelys sneakers. Her red spring curls bounced and swayed around her round freckled face and large ocean blue eyes. She resembled those girls from the 70's roller derby movies. Brittany wore a fuchsia cut off shirt exposing her belly button, and tight jeans, which caused a muffin-top fold over the daisy duke shorts. She made a curve when she arrived at the door and came to a complete stop.

It wasn't that long ago that Brittney dressed like an Amish maiden. If you saw flesh showing, it was her face and fingers. Then about two summers ago, her dad was killed in a car accident. After that, everything went haywire. Her mother started drinking and Brittany fell to the wayside.

Inebriated with freedom, she changed. Brittany opened the door, came inside and rested her elbows on the counter. Her eyes widen; the edge of Brittany's bottom hung below the edge of the jeans. Brittney inflated the gum and popped it.

Her eyes traveled up and down Brittany's body.

"Did your mother see you before you left the house?" Anya asked, as she pointed at her bottom.

Brittney swiveled her head. "My mother is too busy nursing a liquor bottle to notice these cheeks." She slapped her bottom and outlined her body with her hands.

Anya rolled her eyes. "Whatever." She had no desire to show her giggly parts. Anya was comfortable wearing casual vintage tops with fitted jeans and wedges or ballet flats.

"Do you want to go to the ice cream parlor later? Todd will be there."
Brittany raised her eyebrow, smirked and slightly nodded her head.

"Eww. He was here earlier exposing himself."

Brittany laughed, "He's so hot. I'd date him, but he likes you." She frowned.

"I can't go. I have a research paper to finish."

Mrs. Berry's looked over the top of her readers that hung above her strong Roman nose as she stood behind the counter. The wrinkles on her face likened to the grooves on the bark of a tree.

"Hi Mrs. Berry."

She walked to the back of the store without replying to Brittney.

Mrs. Berry climbed up and down the ladder set against the shelves. She traipsed through the aisles in a hideous lace-collared, black floral dress.

"Nice UGGs Mrs. B." Brittney looked at her.

"They're Mary Jane's." She walked to the other end of the store.

"Okay." Brittney held both palms up. "*Those shoes are ugly*," she said in a hushed tone. "She needs a makeover."

"No! You need a make-under." Anya nudged her.

Brittney walked toward the entrance and opened the door. "Suit yourself. See you later." She rolled down the sidewalk.

"It's none of my business, but you might want to choose better company," Mrs. Berry advised.

"She's not so bad," Anya lied.

"If you say so, but I've heard some things—."

"Anya, I'd like you to call the number on the index card by the monitor. Let him know the book has arrived and our store hours."

Anya glanced at the phone and exhaled. Mrs. Berry used an antique rotary telephone for the store; it took forever to dial numbers. She dialed each number clockwise and waited for it to return counter-clockwise. After she dialed the last four digits, she exhaled. *This is ridiculous.* She tried to persuade Mrs. Berry to get a modern phone but she always replied, "Antiques never go out of style." She wondered if Mrs. Berry and her father shared a secret kinship. Neither cared to part with their beloved antiques. "Hello. I'm calling from the Rare Finds Bookstore. May I speak to Liam please?"

"Speaking."

"I was calling to let you know your book has arrived. You can pick it up Monday through Saturday between the hours of 10 AM through 8 PM.

"Thank you. I'll stop by sometime this week," he said.

"Okay. Good bye."

Anya worried about Brittany, but she had problems of her own and it all began a month ago. One evening after coming home early from an outing with Brittany, Anya overheard her dad and aunt talking about something that took place in New York City. She playfully sprung out from the hallway and sat down. Once again, Aunt Lynn was wearing tie-die clothing. It seemed she always found a way to include it into her wardrobe. Anya didn't know how, but Lynn had one of the neatest dread locks for someone with blonde hair.

"What are you guys chatting about?" The dining room fell silent except for the kettle whistling in the kitchen. Lynn got up, went into the kitchen and took off the kettle. Her scent lit up the room. The fragrant odor came from the exotic perfumed oils she wore.

Alan looked at Anya before he spoke. "Stuff."

Her father and aunt went on to talk about unimportant *stuff*. The vague response made Anya curious. She left the living room and went to her bedroom. Anya laid on the bed thinking about what she heard and--how tight-lipped her dad was. She made a conscious decision to look into the matter.

Lynn re-entered the room holding a teacup taking care not to spill anything.

"You had the perfect opportunity to tell her." She entered the dining room stirring the remnants of sugar in the base of the cup until it dissipated.

"Before I forget, there was something I wanted to talk to you about."

"What is it?" Alan asked.

"Do you trust me?"

Alan ate what was left of his eggplant parmesan when the fork fell from his grip.

"Okay Lynn what are you up to now?"

"Why do I always have to be up to something?" She took a sip of tea and glanced at him over the rim of the cup.

"You always say that when you're up to something," Alan huffed. "Like the time you pretended to eat a roasted lizard and I followed your lead. For the record, it did not taste like chicken."

Lynn laughed hysterically. "That was child's play. We are adults now."

"What are you up to?" Alan asked with a perturbed look on his face.

"I'd like to introduce you to..."

Alan interrupted. "I'm not interested." He ate the remnants off his plate and took the dishes to the kitchen. Lynn followed behind him.

"You know you can't keep living with a ghost. It's been sixteen years."

"I know you mean well, but there is no one who can take Azalea's place. So please stop trying to set me up with your lady-friends." Alan pressed one hand against the kitchen counter and the other on the refrigerator door. He stared at the tiles.

Lynn walked down the hallway toward the kitchen.

"I was only trying to help."

"Whatever happened to Cassie?"

"She wasn't my type. Cassie was looking for a white-collar man. I'm a blue-collar guy with a teenage daughter. Besides, I didn't give her a reason to stick around."

"Don't downplay your worth. You own a successful business." Alan sucked his teeth.

"There's no need to toot my horn when I have you to do it for me."

"You know what? I'm through with setting you up," Lynn said.

"It's about time you got a clue."

CHAPTER THREE

Heavy showers hit the roof sending thick bands of water off the side of the building. Anya watched the rain streak down the window. The distant sound of lightning echoed through the classroom. The downpour reminded her that life is not always sunny. Mr. Williams cleared his throat and her eyes turned to him.

Every other week, he assigned a project for each student to work on. His assignments inspired her creativity. She rubbed her hands together as she waited for the details.

"I'm going to switch things up a bit. This time I'm assigning group projects."

Her joy fizzled when he mentioned the word *group*. Grunts of dissatisfaction erupted in the room. He wrote the names of the students in each group on the blackboard.

"I want you to meet with your group for the next fifteen minutes."

The sounds of moving chairs filled the room. Anya was paired with two of her least favorite people in the class, Leslie and Todd. Leslie was not so bad as long as you didn't bother her. Leslie always wore her golden blonde hair in a bun that resembled boxwood shrubs. Anya glanced in her direction. Leslie was a promising fashionista but today she wore a hideous maroon crew-neck sweater with blue skinny jeans and maroon ballet flats.

Mr. Williams outlined the guidelines on the blackboard. Each group had to create a fashion shoot and take pictures worthy of a fashion magazine. It was an interesting project, but she wasn't thrilled about the partner system. Each member had to choose a role: photographer, set creator, or model. He looked around the classroom.

"Any questions?" A student in the back raised his hand.

Leslie leaned into Anya, "I'll be the set creator. My pimples are out of control. I can't have that immortalized in a photo."

"That's fine with me." Deep down, Anya was pissed.

"Well, I guess I'm the photographer," Todd said. Anya rolled her eyes.

"I think we should exchange phone numbers so we can share ideas and track the progress of the project," Todd continued.

"We can do that in class." Anya did not intend to give either of them her number.

"Maybe but I doubt he'll allow us to work on the project the entire time," Todd replied.

"He's right." Leslie smiled.

Anya remembered why she disliked her at times. She wrote her number on a sheet of paper from her notebook, tore it in two, and gave it to them. Todd jotted his down and gave it to Leslie. He turned to Anya, "Call me *anytime*."

Leslie gave him a mean glance. The bell rang. Anya hurriedly gathered her books and left the room before they could say another word. For the record, group projects suck. But, Anya felt everyone would do their part. Todd's obsession with her would keep him focused on the task and Leslie's 'need-to-impress' would harness her creativity. Anya had to bring her "A" game. She sat in study hall trying to figure out what the theme should be, what to wear and how to make Leslie agree with her idea. Leslie walked over and sat a seat away at the table.

"Anya, I have an idea about the theme. I think we should go with Hollywood glam."

"You were wearing a gorgeous outfit a month ago. It was Bohemian Chic."

Leslie thought for a moment, "You know what we should do, a Bohemian Chic theme."

"That's a great idea, Leslie."

"Any ideas on where to do the photo shoot?" Leslie asked.

"Downtown maybe?" Anya asked.

"It can work, but we'd have to worry about people walking into the area. It has to be a more remote location." Anya crossed her fingers, and hoped Leslie got the hint.

"Glen Helen Park," they said simultaneously.

"Sweet." Anya danced in her chair.

"What is the color scheme?" Leslie asked.

"I don't know."

"Can you describe the Bohemian Chic clothing I was wearing so that I can have an idea of the look?"

"I can't recall. Google it."

In reality, she saw Leslie wearing everything but Bohemian Chic but she didn't have to know that. The only thing that mattered was a theme that made sense. After all, they lived in a place that personified the sixty's and that was a good thing. The natives were laid back, friendly and few had dreams of leaving for bright lights and big cities. Most would say their 'happily-ever-after' lived here.

Luckily, Anya had a power player on her side. Once she mentioned the project to her aunt, who was a fashion photographer, Lynn offered to loan them her equipment. Anya couldn't wait to get the project completed. It was interfering with work at the bookstore, school, and some other matters she was eager to attend to. There were many questions that needed answers, but for now, they had to wait.

One evening when her father was at work, she looked at the family album. It was tucked away in a box above the hall closet. After viewing its contents, she had a few questions to ask her father. She decided to ask him when he couldn't avoid her. Anya cornered him in the garage while he organized his tools.

"I'm confused."

Alan hoped it wasn't the talk that all single parent fathers dread about girl stuff.

"About what?" He stopped what he was doing and gave her his undivided attention.

"If mom died when I was three months old like you said, why are there no pictures of her with me in any of the albums?"

"Anya—." Alan stood there pressing his lips firmly together. He did not know what to say.

"She was not fond of taking pictures," he said, after a long pause.

"I don't mean to interrogate you, but my intuition tells me something is off here. I'm grabbing at straws, but did she have something to do with what happened in New York City?"

"Whatever happened in New York has nothing to do with you or your mother."

If it were possible, steam would flow from her ears and nostrils. She was young not stupid. Anya knew a lie when she heard one. Besides the busy thoughts raging through her head, the only thing louder was the sound of the cicadas outside. She felt as though she was suffocating from the inside out. If she could climb to the highest point in town and scream from its peak, she would be okay, but for now, all Anya could do was walk off her angst. She left the garage; her feet met the sidewalk with force as she walked down the street. Cars whisked by as she walked down the sidewalk. A car stopped and the driver rolled down the window.

"What are you doing out so late?"

Anya squinted to make out who it was. The street light outlined her bouffant, Roman nose and the raised mole on her chin. The cast of a shadow made her look quite scary.

"Oh. Hi, Mrs. Berry. I needed some fresh air."

Mrs. Berry continued to look at her. "Are you okay?"

"I'm fine."

"Then, why are you crying?"

"It's a long story and I don't want to bother you with my problems."

Mrs. Berry parked her car and turned off the engine.

"I know young people don't like to talk to grownups, but I promise if you tell me what's bothering you, you'll feel better."

Anya walked around to the passenger side, opened the door and sat down.

"I'm tired of being lied to. My dad doesn't think I deserve the truth."

Mrs. Berry held Anya's hand. "I don't think that's true, dear. What exactly do you want to know?"

"I want to know about my mother."

"Ah, I see." The car fell silent.

"I was told my mother died when I was three months old after a blood transfusion."

"That's not true. She died…" Mrs. Berry stopped herself.

Anya looked at her sideways. Her forehead rippled, "What were you going to say?"

"It's not my place to get involved in family matters."

"If you don't tell me what you know, you're no better than my dad." Anya folded her arms. Mrs. Berry held on to the steering wheel.

"Sixteen years ago, an upheaval took place in New York City. Your parents were staying with your aunt in Manhattan, if I remember correctly." She exhaled and adjusted herself in the seat.

"And?"

"Your mother, Azalea went into labor and she gave birth to you. Your father said it was the happiest day of her life when she held you in her arms. That's all I know."

By now, tears were rolling steadily down Anya's cheeks. Mrs. Berry looked at her.

"If I knew more I'd tell you. I'm sorry Anya." Mrs. Berry knew far more than she wanted to admit. It was Adam's mess and he was the only one who could clean it up.

Anya sobbed, and a low growl escaped her lips as she wiped away the tears with her shirt.

"Thank you for telling me the truth." She reached over and hugged Mrs. Berry.

"You know, you really should be getting home." She held Anya's chin and wiped the tears with her fingers.

"I know." Anya opened the door. "I'll see you tomorrow. Bye." She closed the door and walked home.

The closer she got to her house, the further away it seemed. She opened the front door and walked into the dark living room. Anya could see the kitchen light was on so she went into the kitchen. Her dad stood next to the refrigerator pouring a glass of milk.

"Would you like some?"Alan held the milk carton.

"Sure, why not," she said as he poured her a glass.

"I'm sorry about earlier. I was tired and cranky."

"It's okay dad, don't worry about it," she said and sipped from the glass.

"Are you sure? Your eyes look a bit red. It looks like you were crying or something."

"No, I'm going to bed. Good night." She put her glass on the counter and walked down the hallway.

"No kiss?"

She doubled back and kissed him on the cheek.

Anya couldn't fall asleep. She waited until her father turned in for the evening, went to the living room and watched Nick@Nite. Anya fell asleep after a few episodes of Friends but not before indulging in a few drinks. When Adam woke up the next day, he found her contorted body sprawled on the couch. Her hand dangled just above a half-eaten bowl of popcorn.

"Wake up." Her father lifted her hand and Anya's eyes barely opened. "It's time to get ready for school."

Anya regretted staying up late, but she would have been up regardless. She dragged herself to the bathroom to freshen up. Her neck ached from the awkward position she fell asleep in. *It's going to be a long day*. She got dressed and went to school.

By second period, Anya couldn't ignore the urge to use the bathroom any longer. She asked for a hall pass. A trip to the girl's bathroom was an experience that she had to deal with. Someone would always try to strike up a conversation when you were 'watering flowers' or 'laying bricks.' The stalls on both sides were free so she didn't have to deal with that today. When she closed the door, a few girls came inside. One of them spoke by the sink area. Anya peeped through the slits in the joint of the stall and saw Leslie and Amanda.

Once when Amanda was bored in science class, she chewed paper, and poured glue on her hands. Anya was afraid that one day, if Amanda was hungry or bored enough, she'd scarf down the specimens in the glass bottles. Amanda stood in front of the sink holding a tampon in her hand.

"I bought a box. But I can't figure out how to use it," Amanda said. Leslie laughed hysterically.
The sound of Anya flushing interrupted their discussion.

"Read the instructions on the box. It's not that complicated," Anya said as she walked out of the stall. She washed her hands.

"Hi Anya, how's the project going?" Leslie asked.

"Good. Call me later and I'll fill you in." She left them to finish their seemingly pointless conversation.

Mr. Radcliff had a cone shaped head, and it didn't help that he was bald on top. He wore glasses and had an unusual accent. One student blurted out what everyone else was wondering. "Mr. Radcliffe, why do you talk like that?"

It wasn't the first time he heard this question, but over the years, he had learned how to make it a teachable moment.

"I was born in Virgin Gorda." He proceeded to give a speech on cultural exploration. Mr. Radcliffe encouraged them to explore other cultures. His accent did not bother her. She was more concerned about the dead frogs and pigs in the jars. As long as she didn't have to dissect anything, he could speak Korean for all she cared. The final bell rang and she wasted no time getting out of there.

Todd was hanging out with his friends in front of school when Mr. Polanski pulled up and parked near the sidewalk. He looked around. Alan did not see Anya. He saw Todd.

"Hey Todd, have you seen Anya?" Todd approached Alan's car.

"She took the bus."

"Thanks."Alan drove away. He called Anya's job.

"Mrs. Berry, is Anya there yet?"

"No not yet. I'll have her give you a call when she gets in."

"Thanks. Bye."

Anya walked in a few minutes later at the bookstore.

"Anya your dad called."

"Okay."

A customer walked in behind her and went up to the counter. "Can I help you?" Mrs. Berry asked.

"Yes, I'm here to pick up a book, "A Pickle in a Pod."

She picked up the index card and said, "Liam."

"Actually, my name is Ian."

"Sorry, Ian, that will be $9.95."

Anya stood by the first row of shelves in front of the counter with a duster. He looked familiar, but she couldn't put a finger on it. Brittany walked past the store before she turned around and came in.

"Hi Anya. I didn't see you in school today."

"I was there." Anya continued to dust the shelves.

Mrs. Berry finished the transaction.

"Would you like a bag with that?"

"Yes, please."

"Are you new in town?" Mrs. Berry hadn't seen him before.

"Yes, I transferred from a high school in New York a few months ago."

"Well, I hope you like it here."

"Yeah. Got to go, bye."

Brittany gave him an all-encompassing look.

"He's fine."

"You'd say a naked mole rat is cute."

"Did you look at him?"

"Nope!" Anya pretended to have no interest in the matter.

"Anyway, a few of the guys from the color guard invited me to their club house. You want to come?"

"Will other girls be there?"

"I don't know."

"That sounds like a bad idea. You don't know what they have in mind. I'm not going and you shouldn't. Trust me, the last thing you need is to be passed around like a peace pipe." Anya came down the ladder.

"Your presence is needed elsewhere." Brittany was all ears. "I'd like you to be my assistant for a photo shoot project for Mr. William's photography class."

"I'd love to. I'm so excited."

"Relax, Brittany."

Mrs. Berry cleared her throat. "Lower your voices, please."

"When is the photo shoot?"

"The day after tomorrow."

The weather was cooperating. The air was a nice blend of hot and cold. Glen Helen Park was never short of visitors. For some reason, today was low on foot traffic, which was a good thing. The last thing they needed was a random person strolling into the shot. Lynn stood aside and offered Todd some advice. "Pay attention to the source of light and let it work for you, not against you."

Brittany bellowed, "Wardrobe change," She unzipped the garment bag and set out scene two's accessories. Todd heard Anya's teeth tap as they made contact. Her limbs were trembling. Todd put the camera on the back seat of his dad's car and brought over a folded afghan.

"You can use this to stay warm." He unfolded the afghan and draped it over her shoulders.
Anya's face lit up. She glanced at him and smiled.

"All right, let's get you ready for set two," Leslie said. Someone had to keep them on track. "We should add a brighter color to your eye shadow to add dimension and complement your attire," she continued.

"Anya the first shoot was really good. I want our group to avoid over doing it." Todd did the finger quotation gesture, "You know; the constipated, overly sexy, or too methodical look. Let the environment inspire you. Feed off of the things that make you happy or sad and express it in your eyes and body language."

"That's expert advice Todd." Lynn was impressed by his direction. "I could use someone like you as an intern."

"Really? That would be awesome." Todd stood a bit straighter than he did a few minutes ago.

Anya changed into a new outfit and stepped from behind the makeshift dressing room where Brittany and Leslie held a sheet around the back-end.

"I'm ready." Anya twirled.

"Nice," Brittany said with excitement. Leslie looked at her watch.

Anya folded the afghan and gave it to Brittany.

"Hmm actually, it matches with what you're wearing. You can use it as long as you don't hide the outfit," Todd advised from behind the camera.

"That works for me," she replied.

The leather spaghetti-strap, blue, razor back dress, with a three tier ruffled bottom outshone the subtlety of the afghan as it draped around the edge of her shoulders and around the back of the wood chest.

A succession of flashes lit up the front of the camera as he took pictures of her. In the last frame, he got a shot of a butterfly hovering just beyond her auburn curls before a brisk wind blew it away.

"It's a wrap," Todd said as he looked at Lynn.

Lynn looked around the shoot area with her hands on her hip. "You guys did a great job." She gave Todd her business card. "I'd really like to have you as a summer intern. "Thank you."

"Keep in touch," Lynn said.

"I will." He shook her hand and she walked toward the car.

Anya took off the outfit and got back into her regular clothing. Leslie put the outfit on a hanger and placed it over the top of the door.

"What are you doing later?" Brittany put the clothing inside, zipped the garment bag and put it in Lynn's car.

"Work, and afterwards home," Anya replied.

"Come on, it's Friday. Let's go to the roller rink." Brittany wanted to have fun. She'd have more fun if Anya were there.

Anya entered the passenger side. "Okay. Let's do it."

"It's about time. I've been trying to get you to go out with me for over a year now," Brittany said from the back seat. Anya waved at Todd and Leslie.

Lynn started the engine and drove away. Todd followed behind them.

"You all did a great job," Lynn said as she drove away from the park.

Disco tunes from the 70's streamed from the large speakers at the roller rink. Brittany sat at the table and slurped on a milk shake. Anya bit into her burger, a bit of ketchup oozed from one corner of her lip, and she licked it with her tongue.

"So, what's going on with you and your dad?" Brittany put her shake on the table. Anya fiddled with her fries. She dipped a few of them in ketchup and ate them.

"Nothing," Anya mumbled.

"You're talking to me, your best friend since grade school."

"He's been lying to me about my mother."

"What was he lying about?" Brittany moved in closer.

"About how she died," Anya said before she took a sip of her shake.

"Your dad can do no wrong in my eyes. He's been a second father to me since my dad passed."

"You can have him then." Anya rolled her eyes.

"He's been a great dad. If he lied, it was for a good reason."

"Everybody lies, but it doesn't mean it's for the right reason."

"Point taken. Come on. Let's go skate our troubles away." She pulled Anya up out of the seat.

"Then I'll be skating for the rest of my life."
They both laughed. "Go ahead. I'm going to finish my sandwich." Anya sat down. Brittany rolled on the dance floor and put her hands up in the air. She snapped her fingers and swayed her hips to the music.
Roll bounce
About face
Roll bounce

28

Brittany's hips were on overdrive by the time Anya entered the dance floor. They playfully hip-bumped each other, and ran circles around the dancers on the floor.

CHAPTER FOUR

Eduardo sat in Anya's seat when she was in another class. His black hair was faded, and the texture of his hair made him look like a porcupine. He was unnaturally tall for his age and had the shoulders of a linebacker. Each day he'd find new ways to gross her out. He smeared an array of dried boogers on the desk. Anya looked to the right.

Stephanie Rhodes sat two rows across from her. When anyone broke the class rules, she was happy to tattle. Besides telling, she rarely spoke. Students named her Rainbow Bright. Her pink and blue hair sent their imagination into overdrive. Stephanie and Eduardo would make a perfect couple. She sat at her desk during the lecture, leisurely picking her nose and ate her boogers. This would go on until her nostrils were spotless and her craving for the exotic delicacy had subsided. Afterwards, she'd resort to biting her nails. The faint crunching sound irked the teacher after a while and he would stop what he was doing and stare at her. When she stopped nibbling, he resumed the lesson.

For the rest of the period, Anya spent her time decontaminating the desk with disinfectant wipes. She looked at the clock over the blackboard. Every time she looked at it, the short hand seemed to stand still. She was trying to concentrate, but Johnny, who sat in the first-row, fifth seat, kept drumming. He had a mushroom haircut and his neck was super skinny with a huge Adam's apple. His lanky frame reminded her of a praying mantis. Each time he tapped on the desk her anger grew. She fought with the idea of shouting, "STOP," but she also knew Mr. Williams had her dad's number on speed-dial.

The bell rang. She stared intensely at Johnny. He looked over his shoulder and tapped on the desk. She wished she could break his fingers, or smash them 'Misery' style. Shattering his phalanges would surely give the class months of drum-less moments. Thankfully, Johnny was not in her next class.

She couldn't wait to go to photography class. The group assignment was complete and submitted for grading. She was eager to find out the grade they received on the assignment. Mr. Williams walked back and forth behind his desk, twirling a pen in his hand and then cleared his throat.

"I was impressed by the level of sophistication of the photos submitted by this class. You've definitely raised the bar for next year's class." The students clapped and whistled. He put his hand up to quiet them down.

"I emailed a friend of mine at the Yellow Springs News Paper. He would like to interview and showcase the best group pictures on the front page."
Heavy breathing engulfed the room as they waited.

"The best group assignment goes to Todd, Anya, and Leslie."
Anya sat there with her mouth wide open. She looked at Leslie and smiled.

"Yes! We did it!" Todd shouted cocking his elbow to his ribcage while making a fist.

Her classmate's disappointment was eclipsed by their elation. It was slowly sinking in and she displayed a broad smile; something her classmates had rarely seen. Anya wiggled her body in excitement. It felt good to be happy about something for a change. The best part was that it freed up time for her to work on her investigative research. She knew she'd have to start at the beginning to get the answer and she had a composition book half-filled with information.

Anya had sleepless nights and many unanswered questions. She spent her free time at the library, and went through old newspapers on the microfilm-indexing machine, while, her peers contemplated whom they'd ask to the prom. She was glad the school year was almost over. Anya asked her dad if she could spend the summer in New York. At first, He was hesitant, but Lynn assured him that she'd keep Anya engaged as her assistant when she had a photo shoots or with recreation throughout the city.

The newfound fame of having her face plastered all over the Yellow Springs News Paper was flattering at first, but as the town got wind of it, it turned into a whole other matter. Bookstore patrons and random strangers on the street complimented her on the photos. Her father joined the bandwagon. Alan bragged to his clients at his car restoration shop when Anya came around. If she could tune him out she would, but it was impossible. The only thing she was interested in hearing from him was the truth, but he had a comfortable relationship with lies and the truth was a bad omen.

It was Friday and there was an early dismissal. Her dad was at work and she did not have to go to work after school. So, she rode her bike to Clifton Gorge. When she arrived simple trails led her to magnificent views of the Miami River. She walked along a wooden boardwalk, taking in the scenery. Her father brought her there when she was little. He once said that the gorge was a perfect place for people to cry. Their tears would fill the Miami River and wash their sorrows away. When she wanted to cry, she would go there to meditate and contribute to the flow of the river. Holding in all the conflicting emotions for six months had been unbearable. She had to let the tears out before it caused her to combust.

Anya walked along the cleared paths that led to the boardwalk, down to the lower deck and eventually the river. In-between the levels of the wooden boardwalk were steep wood and stone steps. A loud squawk from a hawk that flew over startled her and she missed a step. Anya screamed as she tumbled to the bottom of the steps. She was a few steps away from the bottom. If she were any higher, she would be front-page news for another reason.

A voice echoed from across the river.

"Hey!" He called out. Anya attempted to sit up and fell into a slump. He leapt across the river like an agile child on the elevated rocks and ran up to the base of the steps.

"Are you okay?" He raised her head.

"I think so." He helped her to her feet.

"Hi, I'm Ian Borland. Are you the girl from the bookstore? "I'm a junior at your school."

She looked up at him. "Yes. My name is Anya." She estimated his height at six feet.

"You're that guy who splashed water on me."
Ian loosened his hold on her. She swayed as she tried to put pressure on her left foot.

"I think you've sprained your ankle. I can lift you if it's okay with you?" He extended his hands. When she hesitated he said, "I won't do anything inappropriate, I promise."

"Okay."
He lifted her. Ian walked over to a large mounted stone where visitors often sat to rest their feet from the sometimes-torturous trails and put her down.

"I'm such a klutz." Anya was upset with herself; after all, she came to cry, not to hurt herself.

"Don't beat yourself up. It's steep on that level. Trust me; you aren't the first to trip on the way down. You're just lucky to live to talk about it."

She laughed. "You're right."

"What are you doing out here by yourself?"

"I have issues. I needed to go somewhere to clear my head. Instead, I almost broke my leg."

They both laughed.

"What's wrong?"

"Well, my dad has been lying to me."

"About what? If you don't mind me asking."

"Trust me, you wouldn't understand."

"Everyone has problems. I'm seventeen years old. I lost both of my parents when I was twelve months old.

Actually, I am on the National Database for missing children to this day. The couple who found me reported me as a missing child. They loved me like their own. Eventually, the state allowed them to adopt me."

"I'm sorry about what happened to your parents."

"Thank you, but I've made peace with what happened."

"Well I guess it's my turn." Anya exhaled. "My father told me for years that my mother died after a blood transfusion when I was three months old, but I'm not so sure anymore."

"What are you going to do about it?"

She looked into his pale blue eyes. "Find out the truth."

He smiled. "That's a start. I hope you find all the answers you are looking for."

"I hope so too."

"I'm getting ready to leave. I can help you get to the top unless you have another way to get out of here."

"Nope. I think I'll take my chances with you." He picked her up and carried her to the top of the trail.

"My bike is over there," she said, "how will we do this? How did you get here?"

"I walked. I can tow you on the inner bar. You'll have to keep your legs out of the way." Anya was not thrilled about the idea. The last time she was towed on a bike was by Brittany, and it did not end well. Brittany rode into the back of Mr. Feinstein's car and got them both grounded for a week.

Ian sensed her uneasiness. "We'll be fine."
It was awkward at first, but he managed to tow her home. Alan was outside washing his car when Ian rode up and came to a stop in front of her house.

He stopped what he was doing and walked up to them. "What's going on?"

"I sprained my ankle. This is Ian; he goes to my school. He offered to bring me home."

"Are you okay?" Alan held her shoulder.

She limped as she stepped away from the bike.

"You really shouldn't put pressure on your foot for a day or two." Ian knew what he was talking about; he had endured a few sprained ankles during his early childhood.

He shook Ian's hand. "Thank you, young man for bringing her home safely."

"What's your name again?"

"Ian Borland."

"Borland—. Alan tried to recall where he heard the name. "That name sounds familiar.

Where are you from?"

"Poughkeepsie, New York."

"Wait a minute. What's your folks' name?"

"Jim and Carol Borland."

"Well I'd be damned, I know them. We met sixteen years ago in New York City."

Anya's ears perked. She looked at Ian and then at her father.

"You're the baby they found. You probably don't remember me. My wife, Azalea, held you a lot."

It was the first time Anya heard her dad speak of her mother voluntarily. She tuned out all the other sounds and listened.

"It's good to see you are okay. Would you like to stay for dinner?"

"I don't think my aunt, Mrs. Burris would mind. Can I use your phone so I can let her know?"

"Sure." Alan gave Ian his cell phone.

Alan finished washing the car before going inside to prepare dinner.

"Can you eat seafood?"

"No, I'm allergic."

"What about chicken?"

"That's fine."

Alan started working in the kitchen. The aroma of curry, onions, and peppers filled the kitchen. The distinct whistle of the pressure cooker chimed throughout the house.

"Your dad seems like he knows what he's doing."

Anya chuckled. "Yeah. He's had sixteen years to figure it out. There were times when I was in grade school when I told him his food tasted like faux food."

Ian laughed. "You must have been a ball of sunshine."

"Not exactly. Just brutally honest," she replied, smirking.

"Dinner's ready." Alan balanced a plate in each hand placing them in front of Anya and Ian. He walked back into the kitchen to get his plate and returned to the table.

"What are you waiting for? Eat," Anya said.

Ian took a bite of the curried chicken. "It's delicious and tender. This is definitely a treat."

"Thank you. I'm glad you like it. It's the least I can do to thank you for bringing Anya home."

"I did what any decent person would."

Anya got up. "Ian, would you like something to drink? We've got juice and soda."

"A glass of water is fine."

"I'll take water too," Alan replied.

She went into the kitchen.

"How is Jim and Carol?"

Ian waited until he swallowed the food in his mouth. "Not so good. Carol died four years ago. Jim is alive, but two years ago, he developed Alzheimer's. He's in a nursing home in Poughkeepsie."

"I'm sorry to hear that. They were a nice couple. It's a shame we didn't keep in touch."

Anya walked into the dining room and put the glass of water next to Alan and Ian then went back into the kitchen. Anya stood in the hall listening to them and paused before entering the dining room.

"My life was perfect before that—." A haunted expression came over his face.

"I lost a piece of myself." Alan shook his head and looked away. He realized his recollection was changing the mood in the room.

"I'm sorry. I couldn't help myself. Meeting you just brought the past into the present."

"I'm sorry. Maybe I should leave." Ian eased his chair away from the table.

"Please stay. I'm glad you're here. I always wondered what happened to you."

When dinner was over, Ian and Anya sat on the front porch.

"That was awkward." Anya wasn't sure what to make of her father's admissions during dinner.

"Your dad is nice. I hope you can move beyond whatever differences you have with him."

"Anything is possible. I'm curious." She hesitated and went silent.

"About what?" Ian asked.

"You said you were raised by a couple in New York?"

"Yes, the Borland's. It's a long story, but I live with his younger sister, Mrs. Burris now. I should go. I don't want her to worry. I'll see you later." She waved as he walked down the street.

When the evening slowed down, Anya thought about what Ian and her father discussed. She decided to dig for more information on the Newyork.gov website. Maybe she could find out more about her mother's death. After looking through numerous links, she found a mailing address to request information.

CHAPTER FIVE

It was a week before prom, and the students who had dates couldn't stop talking about what they were going to wear or who they were going to prom with. Unfortunately, students like Anya, who planned to go alone, weren't in the best of spirits. Students who asked someone and were turned down, evaded the topic all together. Anya had a few offers. Eduardo was the first to ask, but that response was hell no with sugar on top. The last thing she wanted to do was sanitize each time he touched her with his *Boogie Night*s fingers. Then Todd chimed in, but Anya let him down easy. She told him that since she knew Leslie liked him she couldn't go with him.

Johnny the drummer asked Brittany to the dance, and she accepted his offer, but she thought Brittany could do better. She envisioned Johnny going into Kanye mode. He'd go up on stage, take away the drummer's sticks and burst out into a drum solo.

On the night of the prom, Brittany came over to Anya's house. She offered to help Anya get ready. Anya had the task of taming Brittany's wild red hair into a ponytail. Brittany found a turquoise dress lined with black lace with a drawstring back. It would go nicely with her mild olive undertone. By the time Anya finished putting eyeliner and mascara on Brittany's eyes, she looked breathtaking with a hint of light-silver and medium-grey eye shadow. She left the room so she could get dressed. When Anya returned, Brittany looked like a young version of Dolly Parton with her breasts peaking just above the bustier-like dress.

"You look beautiful," Anya said as she held Brittany's shoulders.

"Where's your dress?" Brittany looked around the room.

"In the closet, but I'm not going." Anya sat on her bed.

"You can't leave me alone with Johnny," Brittany said.

"Yes I can. He's harmless unless you're a desk."
They both giggled.

"Please come." She gave Anya her best puppy face.

"Okay give me a few minutes." Anya gently pushed Brittany out of her room and closed the door.

Anya worked on her makeup. She looked through her dresser for a strapless bra, put on the dress, and zipped it up halfway.

"Can you zip this up for me?" Brittany waited outside her bedroom and opened the door.

"You look like a movie star."

Anya turned around. "Zip it up for me please." Anya was dressed in a black strapless dress with a cubic zirconium appliqué in the middle of the bustline and cubic zirconium accent strapped heels.

"You're going to break a few hearts tonight." Brittany zipped the back of Anya's dress.

They walked into the living room where Alan was watching TV. "Dad, we're ready."

"Oh my, you girls look so beautiful."

"Thanks dad."

"Thanks Mr. Polanski."
Alan got up. "Okay then, let's go."

On the drive to Yellow Springs High School, it was mostly quiet with the exception of the sound of the wind cutting through the car.

"It wasn't that long ago you two were playing in the front yard, riding your bikes or playing hop scotch. Now you're on your way to prom." His voice cracked when he spoke.

"It's not the end of the world, dad. We're going to a dance. Graduation and college are a long way off."

"True." He regained his composure. Alan pulled up in front of the gymnasium.

"Have fun, but be safe."

"We will." Anya kissed her dad on the cheek while Britt got out and waited outside the car.

"I'll pick you guys up at midnight."

The gymnasium was decorated with fringe, strobe lights, and fake palm trees. The music was pumping. Anya felt the vibration from the large speaker. The gym was filled, but no one was dancing. The students stood in a large social circle waiting for someone to be the first to bust a move. The better the music got, the smaller the circle became. Slowly they moved from side to side, shimmied up and down until the circle dissipated. Everybody on the dance floor was doing what they did best. Some were popping and locking and others were doing the latest dance craze. Brittany was having a blast dancing with Edward. She tried to pull Anya on the dance floor, but she declined. Anya stood by the wall. The DJ switched up the music and put on Rock and Roll. Anya started swinging her hair and playing the air guitar.

"Nice skills." He walked up and stood beside her. She looked to her right to see Ian dressed in a white tuxedo with a red scarf tucked in the pocket. His black spiked hair was slick at the sides and the top flipped backward.

She giggled, "Not exactly."

"You look beautiful."

"Thank you, you look nice too. It's nice to see you in a color other than black."

"Would you like to dance?" He extended his hand.

"Sure."

The music changed and a slow song came on. Brittany saw Anya enter the dance floor and gave her a thumbs up. Ian put his hand at the side of her waist, held her hand, and led the dance. She looked up at him and he looked at her. The song progressed as she rested her head on his chest. Shortly after, Anya felt a tap on her shoulder and looked back to see Todd standing there.

"May I have this dance?"

Anya saw Leslie trailing behind him. She walked up and stood next to Todd.

"I'm sorry, I can't."

The expression on Leslie's face changed from confused to perturbed. "How *could* you? I'm your date!" She stormed out of the gymnasium. Todd walked off in the opposite direction.

"What was that about?" Ian asked.

"I don't know."

"Would you like something to drink?" Ian asked.

"Sure. I'll come with you."

He got a glass of punch for them. They walked over to the bleachers and sat down. Ian stole occasional glances when she was not paying attention.

"What are you doing for summer vacation?" he asked.

"I'll be staying with my aunt in New York."

"And you?" Anya asked.

"For the first three weeks I'll be here, but in July, I'll go to Poughkeepsie to visit my dad."

Sir Mix-a-Lot's song, Baby Got Back came on. The students all cheered on the dance floor.

"This is my song," Anya smiled from ear to ear.

Ian looked at her and shook his head.

"Let's go." He held out his hand, she placed her hands in his, and they walked unto the dance floor. Before they knew it, they were dancing up a storm. The students seemed to be getting the hang of the prom. Girls with no "Butts" started backing up their flat booty sacks every time the line "Baby got back" came up and a few guys pretend to smack their bottom as they danced. When Anya and Ian finished dancing they were sweating.

"That was fun," Ian said.

The principal walked on stage and spoke into the microphone, "I hope you've all had a great time this evening. The prom will be ending promptly at midnight. Get home safely and have a wonderful weekend, good night."

He walked off the stage. Anya leaned in and whispered in Ian's ear, "I have to go. My dad will be here in about 10 minutes."

"I'll walk you out."

Anya signaled by pointing to her watch. They walked outside to the front of the gymnasium. Brittany said good-bye to Johnny and walked toward the exit.

Ian cleared his throat, "Can I have your phone number? So we can keep in touch over the summer."

"Sure, why not," Anya said. Brittany walked up and stood beside her.

Ian took his cell phone out of his pants pocket, "Okay, what's your number?"

Brittany cleared her throat and gave Anya a googly-eyed look. He entered her number into his phone book.

Alan spotted them standing among other students, waiting. He pulled up, "Good evening Mr. Polanski."

"Hi, Ian."

Anya got in, and Brittany got in the back seat. She waved at Ian as Alan drove off.

Anya couldn't wait for school to end, and now that it had, she missed it. She endured a week of working full-time at the bookstore before it was time to leave for New York. Anya looked above the coach cabin for her seat number. She had a window seat, which was great, except for the fact that she was afraid of heights. Anya kept the shutter closed. A portly woman walked through the aisle, bucking the seats as she walked by, and sat next to Anya. When she sat down, her stomach and breasts became one.

"Hello, what's your name? My name is Agnes."

"Anya."

"You're a pretty young lady."

"Thank you." Anya opened the shutter. The baggage handlers were still loading the luggage in the luggage compartment. Agnes reached for a book out of the pouch from behind the seat. She flipped through a magazine. The cargo hold was sealed and the luggage car drove away from the plane. The plane reversed and taxied down the runway. It waited in a succession of other planes for permission to take off.

Finally, it was their turn. The plane traveled down the runway, made a hard right and bolted down the tarmac. Anya felt like a sailor was tying knots inside her tummy. When the plane left the ground and soared diagonally into the sky, air pockets lodged in her ear. She pulled out a stick of gum and chewed it. The sound of the wheel folding up followed by a thump when the wheel well closed unnerved her. The plane rattled when it pierced through clouds to reach its cruising altitude.

At first, it sounded like a racecar revving the engine, then a low moan followed by a loud snort. Anya jerked to attention and looked to her left. Agnes was fast asleep breathing noisily and it overpowered the sound of the air being pumped into the cabin. Her head rose and lowered into her bosom as she inhaled and exhaled. Luckily, the flight was only two hours long, and forty-five minutes had already passed. The only time the passengers got a break from her snoring, was when the flight attendant came through the aisle with the food cart.

"Chicken or fish?" The flight attendant asked Agnes and then Anya.

"Fish." Agnes replied.

"And you, young lady?"

"Chicken."

By the time Anya took a bite of her chicken, Agnes's plate was clean. Her plump cheeks lay like bunkers as she frowned.

"I can't believe they gave this tiny plate of food to a grown woman." She shook her head.

Agnes stared at Anya's plate. Anya realized her interest and adjusted her seat. She could see Agnes closing in from the corner of her eye. Anya swiftly ate her food and washed it down with juice. The flight attendant came through the aisle collecting garbage. The 'fasten seat belts' sign came on a few minutes before the flight attendant finished collecting the trash and strapped the food cart in place. Another flight attendant checked the overhead compartment by sliding her hands over the doors from the back of the plane to the front. Then she sat in the chair behind the cockpit and fastened her seat belt.

Anya couldn't recall what was worse, departure or descent, although she might choose descent. The thought of fighting motion sickness, the illusion of landing on a building or water, while fighting air pressure in her eardrum wasn't exactly the most desirable situation. She held on to the hand rest for dear life as they descended. The plane couldn't land quick enough as far as she was concerned. When the tires met the tarmac with a screeching sound, it was music to her ears until they began to accelerate at what seemed like the speed of light. Her heart seemed to propel to the back of her throat.

The plane slowed down and the sound of applause filled the cabin. A woman in the next aisle made the sign of the cross on her chest, kissed her pendant, and then placed it back in the confines of her bosom. Anya looked to her left. Agnes was once again snoring in soprano. Anya nudged her. "We have landed."

"Thank God for that," Agnes said. Drool spilled from the corners of her lips as she straightened her clothing.

Anya smiled, turned to the window, and slid the blinds up. She looked out the window as they taxied into the terminal. The pilot waited for a few minutes before turning off the 'fasten seat belt' signs. Passengers got out of their seats, retrieved their carry-on from the overhead compartments and waited for the walkway to be attached to the plane. The line moved slowly at first but the pace increased once half of the passengers exited the plane.

Anya walked through the tunnel and past numerous terminals to the baggage claim area. She could see her aunt standing at the end of the waiting area adjacent to the baggage claim. Anya walked toward her pulling her carry-on bag.

"Hi." Anya hugged Lynn and she kissed her on the cheek.

"Welcome to New York City."

"We're going to have so much fun. I'll take your bag." Lynn took the handle of the wheeled luggage from Anya and they left the lobby.

CHAPTER SIX

The view of the Hudson River from the Staten Island Ferry was one of the free guilty pleasures in New York City. A ride on the ferry provided many delights. One of them was a view of Lady Liberty. Whether near or far, the Lady left an indelible impression on sightseers. The sea breeze brushed against Anya skin. She was working up the nerve to open a letter she'd gotten a week before she came to New York. She sat on a bench on the upper level balcony. Anya took the envelope out of her messenger bag.

New York State Department of Health, Vital Records had responded to her request for a death certificate. She felt like a coward for not opening it sooner. It's strange how one can be uncomfortable with lies, yet fear the truth. Today she planned to face the truth head on. Her hands trembled as she broke the seal and took out two sheets of paper. 'Enclosed is a copy of the death certificate you requested. If you have any questions please contact our office at the following number.'

Anya separated the first page from the second page. She carefully examined the document. 'The cause of death: Placental Abruption; hemorrhage. Date of death: August 6.' Anya was born on August 5. Her breath hastened. Anything that happened after was a blur but she managed to make it home in one piece.

Her cell phone rang. The key pad lit up in the dark bedroom. She looked at the caller ID. The number was familiar so she answered. "Hello."

"Did I catch you at a bad time?" Ian asked.

"No. I'm having trouble falling asleep."

He sensed something wasn't quite right. "What's bothering you?"

"A lot and it would take all night to tell you."

"I have all the time in the world."

A few moments went by without a response, so he moved on.

"I want to come to the city sometime next weekend. Will you be busy?"

"I don't think so."

"If you're not busy we can go sightseeing."

"Sounds like a great idea." The phone went silent.

"I'm a good listener. Whatever it is you can tell me. What you tell me will stay between us." Ian broke the silence but a long pause followed.

"I found out my mother died the day after I was born, not three months later as my father claimed."

"I'm glad you cleared that up, but something tells me you're not satisfied."

"I don't know, Ian. Throughout this whole thing, a sickening feeling was growing in the pit of my stomach. I thought it was enough to know how and when she died.

"In my dad's papers I found my mother's pregnancy diary. She wrote my due date on it. I wasn't due until the first week in September."

"I can't help but wonder if what happened sixteen years ago had anything to do with it."

"Sometimes when you can't change things you have to accept them." Ian was trying his best to comfort her. "Move on with your life."

"I can't. It won't let me." She cried. "Last night when I was asleep, I saw the image of a fetus on an ultrasound machine. The fetus ripped and clawed its way through the mothers flesh. I woke up when I saw the birthmark. It was *my* birthmark."

"I don't know what to say. That's creepy. I'm here for you if you need me."

Anya braved the subway to go to the library. The subway system was the fastest way to get to any location in the City. There was a lot to deal with while using the subway system; strong perfumes, expired armpits or the stench of cigarette smoke that clung to their clothing. During the less congested travel times, riders were subjected to singing and dance performances. Despite all of the distractions, it was the best way to get around town. The hardest part of using the subway was riding during rush hour. Hundreds of straphangers packed like sardines in a can. Strangers stood face-to-face in an uncomfortable mix of no personal space coupled with being squeezed by other passengers as the train meandered the tracks. It wasn't the most pleasant experience, and at times, it could prove harmful to your health.

After all, according to the evening news, there was a predator on the loose. A man with a foot fetish licked a few women's toes and tried to fondle them while they slept on the train. Anya could not get pass the licking part. With the amount of dirt and grime a person could accumulate at any given time a day, it was hard to comprehend why someone would find that appetizing. Women swore off wearing sandals until the culprit was apprehended. Thankfully, they caught the assailant a few days ago when a woman beat him with her stiletto. Women throughout the city celebrated the fact that they could set their toes free by wearing sandals the next day.

"The next stop is 40th street," the automated announcement said. Anya got off at the 40th Street/Time Square stop and walked up the stairs. When she arrived at the top, she saw a tall, well-dressed, slender man in a black tailored suit and top hat with a large portfolio in his hand. He looked like he had just stepped off the cover of the New Yorker magazine.

Anya crossed the street and walked to 5th avenue. The towering stairs that led to the library entrance rose above eye level. Sitting on the steps a few feet away was a homeless man wearing a dirty pirate hat with three dogs at his side. One mutt sat with his nose high in the air, and a beagle covered in mange laid on its side. The other dog laid on his spine airing out the family jewels. The homeless man paid little attention to the library patrons entering and exiting the building, or the people who passed on the sidewalk unless they tossed money in the pan at his feet. Anya walked up the steps. A low growl came from one of the dogs; she hastened her steps. Anya made it to the top of the stairs and entered the library.

She was able to gather a treasure trove of information from the library. Anya was dumbfounded that no one was arrested for the crime. In the initial attack, 1,970 people were killed. In the aftermath, an additional 1,057 people died. Many arrests were made on that day and weeks following the attacks. Burglary, assault, arson, rape, and loitering were the dominant arrests. With an exception of the latter, the other crimes normally took place whether there was a major attack on the city or not. So, she focused on the arson and loitering arrests.

She had a productive day at the library. The information she gathered made her thoughts heavy. Anya lay in bed looking up. The ceiling was decorated with glow-in-the dark stars. She felt as though she was sleeping under the heavens. It reminded her of the times when she was little and couldn't sleep. Her dad would take her out to the back patio and tell her bedtime stories. He called a few times, but she hadn't returned his calls. Anya missed her father, but she couldn't get over him lying to her.

CHAPTER SEVEN

Alan was lucky he was able to bury his wife, even if he didn't think so. Some families did not have the luxury of burying a body. Their loved ones were reduced to ashes. Their flesh had long decayed and their loved ones hearts ached. Anya made a promise to her mother she wouldn't give up.

Lynn was working late and Anya tried to entertain herself. The walls felt like they were closing in on her. She decided to leave the apartment. The sky darkened as she walked up the block. The streets were never void of people, no matter the time of day. Anya entered a pizzeria. A tall slender woman greeted her and took her to an available table in the corner. The pizzeria was quaint and tastefully decorated with soft red lights against the brick walls, and white lights hung low above the tables.

She sat there looking over the menu. At a table in front of her, two men sat engaged in conversation. A waiter approached her table, took her order, and walked back to the counter. He returned a few minutes later with a glass of water with a slice of lemon. Anya sat there sipping on her drink as she waited for her order.

The voice of a man whose back faced her got louder. His back took up half the seat so she couldn't see past him. The back of his neck looked like a pack of sausages. His salt and pepper hair was thinning and slicked back.

"How are you enjoying your retirement?" The man seated in front of him asked.

"Not too good. I have an unsolved case that haunts me to this day. There isn't a day that goes by that I don't see the faces of the victims," the retired detective said in a thick Bronx accent.

"Dave some cases are difficult to solve." Louis, the off-duty officer said.

"You wear the badge, you do the work." Dave's tone hardened with each word.

"Fine; so what have you done about it?" Louis asked.

"I went to the sergeant about my concerns, but he shot me down every time. He said the case was being handled by the FBI and Homeland Security."

"I think you should let it go."

"It's easy for you to say." Dave elevated his voice. Louis was about forty and wore a fitted blue shirt and a shoulder gun holster that drew attention to his muscular arms. His hair color bypassed red and could qualify as orange.

"You weren't an officer until a few years ago. When you've seen what I've seen, then we can talk." Dave flung his fork across the table.

"I'm done with trying to save you from yourself." Louis dropped his napkin, took out his wallet, dropped a twenty-dollar bill on the table and left the restaurant.

"Excuse me." Anya eased her way to his table. "My name is Anya. I overheard your conversation with the man about what happened sixteen years ago. I'm doing a research paper about it." Dave had a Tom Selleck mustache, but he didn't have his good looks. Scar tissue covered his cheeks and chin.

He gripped his forehead with his thumb and index finger.

"What do you want kid?" He put a fork full of lasagna in his mouth.

"For starters, what did you find out?" She asked with a pen and pad in hand.

"The last week in July, I noticed a group of people around Manhattan distributing flyers. It was no big deal. Someone is always handing out papers to sell you things. But what got me thinking is that when I was in the Bronx, they were there too. They were like locusts everywhere. One day when I was leaving for work, a man was handing out fliers outside of my building, so I took one."

"What was it?" Anya asked.

"The usual mumbo jumbo. I crushed the paper into a ball and tossed it in the garbage."

The waiter walked up to her table. "I'll take my order over here." He walked to the table and placed a platter with pizza in front of her. She took a slice and bit into it.

"We got a few complaints from business owners about loiterers bothering customers. At first, I figured, it's a big city; millions of people are standing somewhere at any given time.

When the attacks happened, and no one took responsibility. It was strange." He moved his hands slightly above the table.

"In the hours and days after the attacks, the same groups popped up around town with signs. It seemed odd to me. I tried to talk to the sergeant about it. Instead, he blew me off. He said, 'I should take some time off.' I did but months later I went back to him. He gave me the statistics speech about how many rapes, robberies, and murders that take place in the city." He said, 'I should focus on those crimes.' "I never brought it up again. I didn't want to make waves. I started drinking, and everything went downhill from there."

"I'm sorry you had to go through that." Anya saw the pain in his eyes.

"Thanks kid. I retired two years ago. I've been sober for a year." Dave shook his head, "but I still can't shake the feeling that I failed those people who died that day and in the weeks following the attacks."

Anya looked him in the eyes, "Can you recall the name on the flyer?"

"New—something. I tried to find out later, but the records were sealed."

"You might find what you're looking for in the arrest records. A few of those people who distributed flyers were arrested."

It was a difficult summer thus far. Ian spent the better part of the summer, visiting with his father at the nursing home. Seeing his dad unable to perform simple tasks, or even acknowledge who he was, was hard to digest at times.

Those 'when I was a child' stories your elders talked about, that made your ears want to hibernate until the story's over after you've heard them a few times, just kept coming. It was one of the interesting dynamics of Alzheimer's. Jim would remember certain events in his life and other memories were filtered and recycled into mush. Those confused moments only served to upset him. It was a good day so far. Jim appeared to be in good spirits.

"I don't remember you being this tall." The last he remembered, Ian was a preteen boy playing around on the ranch. Jim patted Ian on the shoulder. You've grown into a handsome young man." Jim looked around the room.

"I don't like it here. When is Carol coming to get me?"

It was the hardest part of their visits and once again, Ian would have to be the one to tell him.

"She died four years ago."

Jim's face softened. He stared off into the other side of the room.

"That's right, I miss her so much." The cusps of his eyes filled with water. He wiped away the tears with the back of his hand. "I used to love watching her paint in the morning. She was so talented."

"Have I ever told you about our 30th anniversary?"

Ian sifted through the memories in his head. If he had, he would pretend it was the first time to ease his father's nerves.

"No."

CHAPTER EIGHT

Sixteen Years Ago

There was only one thing Carol enjoyed more than a cup of coffee in the morning, and that was painting. She took a short walk to the river below their ranch and set up an easel. She spent the cooler part of the morning absorbing the landscape and painted her interpretation.

To the world, it was just another day but today was a special day for the Borland's. Carol hoped the day would be filled with pleasant surprises and lasting memories, minus the disappointments that can come when ones expectations are set too high. Being with Jim, you never knew what you would get. Sometimes he got things right, and at other times things would go horribly wrong.

A stroke of the brush created trees, which towered and clustered into the Poughkeepsie, New York skyline. Dried leaves sailed on the river as the wind whistled through the trees, adding dimension to the landscape. Sunrays dimmed and invaded the void spaces between the leaves. By the time Carol was finished, a matte painting of shrubs and trees reflected splotches of color on the surface of the river. It all came to life on the canvas.

She smelled the musky residue of her husband's aftershave from the night before, as the morning dew fell around him. The weight of his feet crushed leaves with each step. The side of his face pressed against her cold cheek. Jim placed a thermos on the small table beside her and embraced her from behind.

"Brought you coffee," he said.

"Thanks, Dear."

"I don't know which I like more; the scenery, or your precise representation of it. But I'm partial to you." Jim loosened his hold on her. Carol ran her hand across his face, paused at the cleft in his chin, and rubbed her thumb in its depth.

Jim glanced at the painting once more, and a line of perfect teeth appeared. "I'm going home."

Along the ambiance of the river, Jim drove their minivan on a side street and exited on a dirt road. A wooden sign with the name *Borland Ranch* etched on it swayed from a pole at the entrance of the property. Clouds of dust trailed behind the van as it traveled up the dirt road. Inside the fence, horses trotted and cattle dotted the landscape. Jim Borland walked over and stood in front of the post-and-rail fence at the entrance of his ranch. He waved at his neighbor, riding on a horse in the distance. His neighbor rode toward him, stopped at the fence and dismounted.

"Morning Chuck."

"Good morning. How's the wife?" Chuck asked.

"All right. Today is our 30th anniversary," Jim replied.

"Happy anniversary."

Jim shrugged his shoulder and exhaled. "The jury is still out on the happy part."

"Last year, I had everything planned. I snuck up behind her in the kitchen and said, happy anniversary. She turned around to see me holding a watermelon wrapped in a bow."

His excitement fizzled when he saw the look on his wife's face. In hindsight, it was a lousy idea, but he spent months nurturing the melon in his garden and gave her the best of his crop. It was a prized possession. He thought it would be nice to share it with the love of his life.

Jim noticed Chucks face turning red. Chuck tried to stifle his laughter.

"It's okay let it out, Chuck."

Chuck didn't waste any time. He laughed so much that his horse neighed and thrusted its head up.

"Sorry Pal, but I couldn't help myself."

He looked at Jim and smiled. *Poor fella. He should know by now that food, or anything related to household duties is a no-no.*

"So how did that work out for you?"

"She laments about it every chance she gets." Jim nudged his head. "This time, I'm going to get it right."

Chuck tipped his hat. "Good luck. I have to get back to the house." He mounted his horse and galloped up the field.

Jim walked past the shed toward the house. He saw his wife walking up the road leading to the ranch with her supplies and painting in hand. Jim sat on the rocking chair on the porch. Carol walked up the steps of the porch, set up the easel, and placed the painting on it.

"It looks like it's going to be a nice day, Jim."

"Yes. I want to go to Manhattan today. We should get ready, so we can beat the lunch hour traffic."

Jim and his wife dined at a quaint bistro on East 50th Street. The low ceiling and dimmed lighting added to the relaxed atmosphere.

"Your best bottle of champagne, please," Jim requested. The waiter brought over a chilled bottle, opened it and poured them both a glass. Jim held his glass up, "Happy Anniversary." Carol's glass clicked his, "To many more years," she said.

"The food is absolutely delicious and the portions are generous," she said. "How did you find out about this place?" She preferred her home cooked meals, but this was a treat.

"A colleague told me about it a while ago. I thought I'd give it a try."

"I'm afraid I'll have to adjust my pants after this," Carol said.

Jim laughed. She wiped her mouth with a napkin, placed it on the table and Jim put his hand up to get the waiter's attention. "Check please."

He placed the payment in the leather folder. They left the bistro and strolled to the van.

"Uhh…I am stuffed," she said with a sigh. "We're not done yet." He kissed her hand. "One more stop, after that we can go home."

Jim drove to Central Park. The closest parking spot he found was on Amsterdam Avenue. They walked three blocks to the park. Jim held his wife's hand as they entered the park on 79th Street. The trees were busy as the wind sifted through the leaves, and filtered through Carol's blonde/silver pixie-cut hair. Carol felt comfortable in a fuchsia wrap dress and gold-accent sandals and Jim looked cool in a cream fedora, white Havana shirt, and dress khaki pants. They walked under a series of bridges before arriving at the boardwalk by a pond.

"I have something to show you." Jim stood at the ledge and pointed. Below the ledge, a gathering of turtles in various sizes swam in murky green water.

"It's beautiful. I've never seen so many in one place."

"I thought you would like it since you're always buying turtle ornaments."

She hugged Jim. "Thank you." He loosened his grip on her, reached into his pocket and retrieved a satin box. "I'd like to thank you for 30 wonderful years. I hope to enjoy many more with you." Carol's eyes watered as he placed a pearl ring on her finger. She stared at the ring, "It's beautiful. Thank you." She held the sides of his face and kissed him.

"Eww, mom, their kissing," a little boy said as he walked on the boardwalk with his parents.

"Shh," the mother whispered as she leaned over, and placed her index finger on her lips.

Jim and Carol passed the family and left the park through the entrance where they had entered. While waiting for the light to change, Carol's saw a gallery up ahead.

"Jim, I would like to go to the gallery on the other end."

"Sure, and I'll take a look in the bookstore on this side."

"I'll come over to the bookstore when I'm finished." They crossed on the right side of the street together. Then Carol waited at the crosswalk to cross to the other side. Jim walked ahead and went into the bookstore.

It was a milestone in a young couple's life. Soon they would be responsible for a life other than their own. They entered the ultrasound room. Bland walls and a baby green curtain with a funky cube design hung from the ceiling and made the room less inviting. A large screen mounted on the wall played the local news but the volume was so low they could not hear it. A smaller screen attached to a long arm was bolted to the wall, and hung over the bed. Azalea undressed and put on the gown. She sat on the bed and waited for the ultrasound technician.

Alan stood in the middle of the ultrasound room twiddling his thumbs while his wife laid on the examination table with her tummy perched in the air. A mischievous smirk appeared on his face as he imagined ways to entertain himself. He stood up and began to sway his body to music that only he could hear.

I'm too sexy for my shirt, too sexy for my shirt, so sexy it hurts.

He inflated his stomach and rubbed it as he often did to his wife's tummy. Azalea looked at Alan, exhaled and laughed, displaying the gap in her front teeth. She would often remind herself that he kept things interesting, even when he would do something embarrassing in public.

His ability to make her laugh or make light of a situation was boundless. They met during her first year at Queensborough Community College. She was enjoying a free period in the library when he burst in and held both doors open. He walked through the library with his shirt tossed over his shoulder. His body moved like an inch-worm crossing the road. He purposely flexed his muscles giving the girls a preview of what they were missing.

The quiet library erupted in whispers from one female student to the other. Within seconds, he was on everyone's radar. He was outdone by the librarian shouting, "get out!"The following semester they shared a class, developed a friendship, and eventually began to date seriously, and they've been together ever since. Alan couldn't resist her hazel eyes, set against her strawberry-blonde hair.

He spun around and placed his index fingers on his nipples, and gently rubbed them while moving his body in an s-motion. In his head, the music was playing loud enough and before long, he sang aloud, "I'm a model you know what I mean, and I do my little turn on the catwalk, yeah on the catwalk, yeah and I shake my little toosh on the catwalk."

He didn't care that his singing was not suited for anywhere but the shower. Just as he was about to do another spin, he noticed the ultrasound technician standing inside the frame of the door with her arms folded. Her curly blonde web of hair hung around her freckled face, out-staged by her vibrant green eyes.

Great! Another man-child. "Am I interrupting something?" the Ultrasound Technician asked.

"Not at all. Carry on." Alan spoke in a fake British accent.

The technician could think of a few men he reminded her of, but she had a test to perform, so she kept a straight face. As she walked toward them, Alan straightened his body, looked at his wife, and fluttered his eyelashes. Azalea burst out laughing.

"Would you cut that out?"

"My name is Brenda and I'll perform your ultrasound."

Brenda gave Alan a peculiar look, squirted gel on Azalea's stomach and then circulated the ultrasound tool. She pointed to the outlined figure on the screen.

"There is your baby. I see 10 toes and 10 fingers."

"Is it a girl or boy?"

"The legs are crossed, so I can't tell."

"Must be a lady then," Alan assumed.

After they left her ultrasound appointment, Azalea had a craving for pretzels. She persuaded her husband it was worth the short walk to the pretzel store.

CHAPTER NINE

An explosion cut through the daily bustle about the city. Millions of shrapnel and shards of glass, wood and plastic particles thrust out like paper confetti and fell on the streets. The hypnotic glow of orange, red, and yellow flames engulfed buildings and cars. Smoke plumed atop a ten-story building. The weight of the top floors collapsed creating a domino effect, crushing the lower floors as it lowered to street level. The impact sounded like a fleet of high speed trains running into brick walls over and over until the building fell apart.

In the midst of things, wounds bled as the souvenirs of the carnage lodged in the flesh of New Yorkers and visitors alike. Bells chimed in their ears. Eardrums ruptured and oozed blood. The shockwave set off a symphony of car alarms. Many stared in disbelief while the mist consumed everyone; others ran with no clear destination. The murkiness in the air decreased visibility to arms length. Soot covered victims ran from burning buildings. Eyes watered as the dust clouds thickened around them. Hands became eyes as they felt their way through the tumultuous streets of Manhattan. Calls for help echoed from hollow places and the resonance of incessant coughs came from every direction.

Jim raised his head off the sidewalk and began to hack up phlegm to clear the grit from his throat.

"Carol." Jim paused and coughed again. "Please Lord," he mumbled under his breath. Jim held on to the wall, stood up and looked around him. The fumes in the air brought on a stifling sensation and his eyes began to water. Jim pulled his shirt up to cover his nose. He was not sure what was going on, but he knew there were casualties based on all the debris around him.

Another explosion occurred in the distance. Jim felt the vibration beneath his feet. He grabbed on to anything within arm's reach. There was nothing to solidify stability so he fell to the sidewalk. *Where are you?* Jim shielded himself in a small doorway to avoid a large group of people running in his direction. *This is my fault... I ruined our anniversary. She'd be safe at home, if it weren't for me.* Herds of people were running in different directions. Some collided and fell to the floor. Their cries for help were silenced when the weight of others trampled them.

Carol inhaled; a nauseating feeling came over her. She propped herself up against the building. A few feet away, Jim scanned the area. He ventured out of the doorway to look for his wife.

"Carol?"

"Over here," she waved through the clouded air. Jim ran over, lowered himself and embraced her. He wept as he held her. "I thought I lost you." Jim kissed her on the forehead.

"You're not getting rid of me that easy." Jim held her and helped Carol to her feet.

"Are you okay?"

"Yes."

The terror was visible on the injured victims' faces. A new heinous reality fueled with fear engulfed the city. The thought of a full-on demolition of the city seemed as real as the rubble on the streets. The Borland's main concern was to get out of the city and back home to Poughkeepsie.

The glass of the pretzel shop imploded, sending glass toward Alan and his wife as they stood waiting for the server to complete their order. The force of the blast thrust them forward before they collapsed on the floor. A few minutes later, Alan regained consciousness and immediately nudged his wife.

"Azalea, are you okay?" She swayed her head before opening her eyes.

He eased his body away from her, stood up and helped her to her feet.

"What just happened?" Azalea held her head.

"I don't know, but it doesn't look good." Blood ran from Azaleas nose. Alan's eyes widened. "Are you okay Azalea?"

"My ears are ringing and your voice sounds electronically altered."

"That's normal under the circumstances. Is the baby okay?"

"Yes. I can feel it moving." Alan felt better once he heard that.

The shop was filled with debris. The server was slumped on the floor behind the counter. Alan jumped over the counter and checked to see if she was breathing. He stood up and shook his head.

"She's dead." Azalea's face went blank.

They looked out the shattered window. Clouds of dust and smoke took over the air. It was clear to them that they shouldn't stay there. They left the pretzel shop. Alan held his wife close to him. They came across a few casualties, things they thought they would never see outside of a movie or television screen. A few people covered in debris looked like stone statues, while others ran. The only thing that hinted their humanity was the white pupils that occasionally blinked as they stared into oblivion. It was clear to the Polanski's that this was more than an isolated incident. Everything around them was covered in debris or on fire.

"We have to keep moving until we can get to a safe haven." Azalea gripped her husband's hand so hard it went numb.

"We're going to be okay. I promise."

Azalea saw someone move in the distance and loosened her grip. "It looks like they made it." She pointed down the street at a couple walking ahead.

The Borland's cautiously walked through the chaotic streets. A man covered in dust sprinted past them in a business suit, drawing their attention to the other side of the street. A little girl stood in place, embracing a pole on the edge of the sidewalk. Carol walked to the other side. Jim reluctantly followed her.

"Carol." She stopped in the middle of the street and turned to him. "I know you mean well, but now is not the time to linger. We have to keep moving. We don't know what's going on."

Carols' face reddened as she pressed her lips firmly against one another. "I can't see a child in need and ignore her."

Jim lowered his head for a moment and then looked at his wife. "I get it Carol. I was not implying you ignore someone in need. I want us to make it out of this alive." Jim wished she would hurry up, but instead she was literally acting as a 'fisher of men.'

"Are you done?" Carol rested her hand on her hip. She looked at Jim. He had to know she wouldn't give up that easily. Once she put her mind to do something, there was no stopping her.

Jim tucked his hands in his pockets. "Let's go." They walked to the other side of the street and approached the little girl.

Alan and Azalea were walking on the opposite side of the street. Azalea kept her eyes on the couple.

"Where are your parents?" The little girl glanced at Carol, lowered her eyes and pointed to the body lying in the gutter in front of her. Her mother's bruised face lay sideways on the asphalt with her eyes open. Carol extended her open hand, "Come with us. It's dangerous out here." She tucked away the warnings taught to her by her parents and took Carol's hand.

"We have to keep moving. The van isn't much further," Jim said.

"They took the little girl with them." Azalea felt uneasy. "Why didn't they wait with her until help came?"

"Honey, I don't know. I just want to get back to Lynn's apartment."

Azalea walked across the street and Alan followed. Despite the searing heat she felt comfortable in the tunic top and bohemian skirt but Alan was sweating up a storm.

"I thought we were going that way?" Alan wasn't sure what she was up to.

"We are going to follow that couple." Alan didn't see the need to go to all that trouble, but the last thing he wanted to do was upset her.

Those who had cars, opted to get out of the city. They panicked, and in no time, the streets were jammed with cars unable to move. Tempers flared, obnoxious horns blew, and obscenities were shouted from open car windows when traffic lights turn green and cars stood still. Fights broke out between drivers when their patience wore thin. Some stood on top cars waving their hands to guide emergency vehicles their way but the sirens got further and further away until they were barely audible. Helplessness became a shared emotion among the survivors. Impatience grew during the hours that seemed like months as the injured waited. In the distance, police and fire sirens overpowered the other sounds.

In the midst of things, dust clouds cleared while the injured waited for help. Eventually, cars were abandoned, and on occasion, drivers left keys in the ignition. Cyclists cruised through open lanes of traffic until they were yanked off their bikes, commandeered by the desperation of others. The Borland's sifted through the chaotic streets and arrived at the van after walking several blocks. Their van was blocked in by a sea of cars stretching for miles.

Jim gripped his forehead. *This can't be happening.* If he had taken her home after lunch, they would be watching a movie or out in the garden. Instead, they were caught in Pandora's Box with no way out.

A homeless man parked his cart while he searched for valuables on a deceased woman. The baby that sat beside her did not bother him. The valuables he stole from the woman lined his pockets.   Jim looked on in disbelief. The baby's jeans were covered in pulverized minerals and dust coated his face.

"Hey! Stop!" Jim shouted as they approached. The homeless man took off running in the opposite direction. The disagreeable aroma of dirt, onions, and urine trailed behind him when he sprinted down the street. The baby, startled by Jim's shouts, cried. Carol knelt and took the pulse of a woman who laid in the gutter beside the toddler. She shook her head. "We can't leave him here. He'll be trampled." Carol looked at Jim with pleading eyes.

Jim exhaled. He looked up and shook his head.

"All right. Let's go."

She exhaled and picked up the boy, and held him close. He used his hands to push himself away from Carol's bosom and reached for his mother. Tears dotted the personalized light-blue t-shirt with his name, *Ian*. An intolerable squealing cry escaped his ever-expanding mouth as Carol walked away from his mother.

"Were blocked. Our best bet is to go to Central Park and wait for the roads to clear."

CHAPTER TEN

They approached an abandoned car with the radio on. They stopped to listen.

"You're listening to Hot 97, playing some of the hottest R&B and Rap in New York. We interrupt the regularly scheduled broadcast to bring you breaking news. *There have been numerous explosions around New York City. The Brooklyn Bridge and the Cross-Bronx Expressway are damaged. The federal Emergency management agency is advising people to find shelter and to stay off the streets.*

"People are wilding out. Cars are twisted and bodies are laid out like shag carpet. This is New York B. So let's be real, it's not known for clean streets. Were used to seeing all kinds of shit on the floor. This is crazy. We need the National Guard up in here before things get live and Kats go buck wild. You feel me? Alright, back to the music." 'Hot 97 FM.'"

Jim and Carol saw clusters of trees leading up to Central Park from blocks away. People were running in every direction. At the end of the sidewalk, a young man in his twenties stood calmly with a sign in his hand.

The sign read, 'The trumpet is sounding. The end is near. Repent before it's too late.'

Screams echoed in the streets. A mixture of pork fat, beef, liver and copper filled the air but no barbeques were lit. Some cars with drivers still inside were ablaze. The stench of death was all around them.

"Those who turn away from him will be written in the dust because they have forsaken the Lord," the man with the sign shouted. A young woman stood beside him shaking a tambourine.

"Come on, let's go," Jim said.

"what are we going to do Jim?"

"Something. If we do nothing were screwed."

The Borland's and the children arrived at the entrance of Central Park.

"Let's get as deep into the park as possible," Jim advised. He doubted whoever was responsible for this whole mess was interested in blowing up foliage. They would be safe there for now.

"I'm thirsty," the girl said as she tapped on his leg. Jim wasn't sure where to find a water fountain but he knew he had to find it fast. He had seen too many parents thoroughly embarrassed after their child embarrassed them. Not following through with a child's request, resulted in an embarrassing cry-fest and his ears couldn't handle any more traumas. He could feel a migraine coming on. Jim visually scanned the area for a fountain.

"Okay, a water fountain is over there. We'll rest for a while there."

She stood on her toes at the fountain to reach the spout and he pressed the lever. Her thirst driven slurps was heard a foot away. Now he knew what a person stranded in the desert sounded like when they finally found water. Jim and Carol stood aside and kept an eye on her.

"What are we going to do with these kids?" Jim exhaled and glared at Carol.

"Why are you whispering?"

"Oh! I don't know, but we have to keep them safe." Carol gently held Jim's hand and rubbed it.

"All right, we should keep moving."

"Can we go to the Belvedere Castle?"

"What do you think about that, Jim?"

"Well, it's probably the safest place around here, but we need—."

The girl tugged on Carol's skirt. "I'm hungry." Jim looked at his wife and rested his hands on his hips. Carol waited for Jim to volunteer. His face soured.

"It's a madhouse out there." He pointed away from the park. "I'm a retired teacher, not a magician."

"Now, that's not entirely true. You have managed to redeem yourself for our 30th anniversary compared to last year."

Jim savored the compliment for a moment, and then he huffed, "Except I managed to get us stuck in this debacle, and besides, this is different."

"We have to get something for them to eat."

"Hmm, let me think. If my memory serves me correctly, there is a Whole Foods Market on Columbus Circle. It's not that far from here. It is about 10 to 15 minutes; less if we were driving."

"Okay. Let's go," Carol said. After walking two blocks, Jim wished he hadn't made it sound so easy; now there was no way around it. They were still full from lunch but they couldn't deprive these poor kids food.

Emergency vehicle sirens blared all around them. Tow trucks hauled away cars that were abandoned in lanes at every turn. It was a good sign if the Borland's' were to ever leave the city in one piece. Emergency vehicles edged closer as the abandoned cars were removed. The sight of fire fighters in heavy gear battling fires under a heat index of 90 degrees was calming, even though the city was unraveling around them. At least someone was doing something to preserve the city.

They arrived at Columbus Circle. Black smoke rose, darkening the sky above the buildings in the distance. A man ran past them, balancing an HDTV on his head when they were about to enter the store. The Whole Foods Market large towering glass mirrored the carnage behind them. Normally, the inside was a picturesque collage of produce at the entrance, but today fruits lay on the floor and the store was ransacked. Unmanned registers made it easy for anyone to take whatever they wanted.

"Carol— Grab what you can," Jim instructed as he picked up a few straggled fruits that fell to the floor. "We have to get out of here."

"Can you hold the baby? My hands hurt," Carol said.

"Sure," he took the baby and put him on his hip.

Looters ran through the store scavenging for survival while a man used a crowbar to pry the cash draw open. A loud blast shattered the large glass windows in front of the store. People scattered in all directions for cover and the baby's cry briefly echoed through the sound of the shattered glass tumbling to the floor. The Borland's shielded them the best they could from the flying glass as the floor moved beneath their feet.

"We have to go," Jim said in a firm tone. He could feel his heart beating against his chest so deeply it resounded in his ear cavity. Carol held the girls' hand and they walked swiftly outside.

"We have to go back to the park." Jim looked in every direction. A woman ran by them pushing a shopping cart filled with clothes on hangers, narrowly missing Carol. Jim pulled her aside to avoid a collision and instead, bumped into a young couple behind him.

"Whoa!" Alan shouted and put his hand between his pregnant wife and Carol.

"Sorry, we didn't see you," Jim sighed. "That was a close one." Jim took off his fedora and fanned himself. The young couple stared at him.

"Come on," Jim said as he walked ahead.

Alan whispered to Azalea. "Let's go; this is none of our business. We can't continue this much longer." He was agitated by her insistence to tail the couple but the last thing he wanted to do was deny his wife the right to follow her instincts.

Azalea cleared her throat. "Are these your kids?"

Jim looked at Alan. "Look, I don't have time for this. We are leaving." The Polanski's continued to whisper back and forth as they walked behind Jim and Carol. Jim stopped and Carol looked on as she waited.

He extended his hand, "My name is Jim Borland. I'm a retired teacher from Poughkeepsie and this is my wife Carol." His hand waited longer than he expected so he dropped it to his side. The stranger finally extended his hand.

"My name is Alan Polanski and this is my wife Azalea."

"Well, it was nice meeting you, but we have to go before something else happens. You can come with us if you like." Jim didn't need any more baggage but he felt it was the least he could do under the circumstances.

"Sure, if it's not too much trouble," Alan replied.

"Not at all." Jim continued to walk. He wished he hadn't encouraged him. Now he was stuck with them. Carol had the potential to go rogue on occasion and these two might join her and have a parade.

"Where are you headed?" Alan asked.

"Belvedere Castle."

CHAPTER ELEVEN

Belvedere Castle was perched in the bosom of Central Park atop Vista Rock. The Victorian Gothic architecture punctuated the importance of the park to society. The arrays of skyscrapers draped in a light fog were the perfect backdrop and Turtle Pond reflected the shameless beauty of the castle. You would think that a dynasty of royals ruled from inside the stone façade, but it was built to mirror high society recreation in Europe. The landscape was once filled with swamps, bluffs and rocky terrain, but they molded the most undesirable terrain into art, and Belvedere Castle was no different.

"If hell is hot like this, I'll take a pass," Jim said. He wiped his forehead with a handkerchief and used his fedora to fan himself.

"Here," Carol gave Jim a bottle of water. "You need to stay hydrated," she said. A mild wind swept through the trees, briefly cooling the air.

"We should rest under the trees for a while." Jim unfolded a tarp that he found under the back seat of the van.

Alan and Carol helped put it in place on the floor but an occasional breeze lifted it. Carol played with strands of her pixie-cut hair.

"I have an idea." Carol straightened the tarp and got up. "The girl can get some rocks to put on the edges to keep it in place."

Azalea supervised as she gathered rocks. She proudly displayed her stones to gain approval before placing them on the tarp. She stepped up to Azalea and gently tugged on her shirt.

"Does Princess Tiana live here?" She pointed to the castle.

Azalea looked at her, "No, Princess Tiana does not live here. What's your name?"

Azalea focused on her blue nickel-sized eyes. Her bangs lay to the side and the rest of her hair fell behind her shoulders. Azalea noticed her uncanny resemblance to an anime character.

"Ilia." She gripped the edge of her skirt and swayed. Despite all of the events of the day, Ilia still managed to think about happier things, such as a child's story, The Princess and the Frog. She made it easy for Azalea to smile under the circumstances.

"Hmm, tell you what, you can be the princess of this castle." The newly appointed princess giggled, brought her hands to her bottom lip, and smiled.

Jim took off his fedora, laid back on the tarp and placed the hat over his face. All they could do was wait for an opening to leave the city. Carol sat next to her husband and leaned against the trunk of a tree. Alan laid back on the tarp and his wife lay against him. Ilia paced back and forth in front of them.

"I'm bored," Ilia said.

Jim tipped the hat. "Can you *spell* bored?" When Jim was a kid, 'bored' was a code word for parents to find chores for you to do.

"No," her bottom lip curled down. Ilia wasn't sure what spelling had to do with being bored. She knew she wanted to be home with her family.

"Well, then you can't possibly be bored."

Carol looked at Jim from the corner of her eye. Sometimes he had the ability to be insensitive, and those were his most unattractive moments.

"Come here sweetie, don't pay him any mind. What do you want to do?" Ilia pointed to a merry-go-round.

"Okay, I'll take you to the playground." Ilia's feet pattered.

"I'll help with her," Alan offered as he got up from the tarp. The Borland's were older, but that did not mean they weren't capable of giving them 'the slip.'

"How hard can it be to handle one kid?" Azalea said. She looked at Jim. His head nodded occasionally from side to side.

"Trust me; you don't want to find out," Jim slurred his words before letting out a yawn and then lifted the hat off his face.

"I'm surprised you can sleep with all that's going on." Azalea couldn't imagine sleeping on anything but a bed in her condition.

Jim eased himself up from the ground. We should check to see if the streets are clear. If they are, we can get out of here. He glanced at his watch.

"The castle will close in a half hour. We should get going," he suggested as he got up. "Get Ilia so we can go. First, I'll check to see if we are still blocked in. Jim walked over to his wife. "Are you okay with waiting here?"

"I'll be fine, go ahead." Carol pushed Ilia on the swing one last time before they left the playground.

Jim walked through the trails of the park toward the street. The roads were somewhat cleared, but his van was blocked in by two lanes of cars. The walk back to his wife seemed longer. On any other day he wouldn't care but being stuck during an assault on the city was not appealing. The mere thought made the hairs on the back of his neck stand up.

"All right, let's go to the castle," Jim said.

They walked up the steep steps to the main entrance and entered through the double glass doors. The design of the wooden gallery made the core visually appealing. Traveling through the hallways, leading up to the main bailey invited the imagination to think of what life would be like as a royal. The staircase on the lower bailey led to the turret and the gift shop.

The group walked past the gift shop and headed toward a spiral staircase. Alan backtracked and entered the gift shop. He browsed through the narrow aisles and looked at the items for sale in the glass case. Alan had an idea, but he had to execute it with stealth precision. On the outside, he looked relaxed but on the inside, his heart was beating in overdrive. *This should be easy*, his inner voice said.   A few minutes later, he returned to the group.

"There you are. I was wondering where you went." Azalea held his hand.

"I made a quick stop at the shop."   The group walked up the parapet walkway overlooking the park. Jim, Carol and the children sat underneath the gazebo, looking out at the skyline and the park below. Ilia stood up and stretched her legs.

"The trees look like a village of broccoli." Ilia said.

Carol nodded her head, "Indeed, it does."

Alan and his wife stood at the other end of the balcony.

"It's beautiful up here." Azalea noticed the hot spots where smoke continued to plume and smudge the air but the smoke could not destroy the view from Central Park. In that moment, Alan sensed that nature was far grander than any force that sought to destroy it.

Alan absorbed the scenery and contemplated a plan. His wife and unborn child were his main concern, but it seemed *her* main concern was the children in the Borland's care. For now, he'd observe. An announcement came over the intercom: *The museum will close in 10 minutes*. We will be open tomorrow from 10 AM to 5 PM unless the governor says otherwise. Jim gathered the group together and they headed down the stairs to the lower bailey and into the hallways leading to the wooden galleries.
Jim rested his hands on his waist, "Does anyone need to use the rest room before we leave?"

Ilia raised her hand.

"I'll take her." Ilia took Carol's hand and they walked to the restroom area. While in the rest room, another message came over the intercom: *We are closing in five minutes.*

Carol and Ilia left the bathroom and rejoined the group. They left the building a few minutes before the employees did and walked down the embankment. Alan lagged behind them, reached inside the gift bag, and took out a pair of binoculars. The employees left the castle. Alan looked through the binoculars pointed at the castle. The manager turned on the alarm system and locked the door. Alan lowered the binoculars. They hung from the attached string around his neck.

He walked down the cobblestone incline and on the grass where the rest of his group waited. Jim walked to him. "Isn't it too dark for bird watching?"

His forehead rippled, the corners of his eyes bunched up, and he tilted his head slightly. Jim turned away.

"The darkness is creeping up on us. We have to find a way to get back into the castle."

"I've got that covered." Alan gestured his hand in the direction of the entrance, "Come on." He wasn't sure what Alan had planned, but he hoped it didn't involve destroying public property. Jim was all for surviving this ordeal, but it had to be without doing anything for which he couldn't forgive himself.

They walked up to the glass door. Alan removed a ring of keys from his front pocket and opened the door. Jim, Carol and Azalea looked at one another with their mouths slightly agape. The alarm system beeped when Alan entered; he input the security code.

"You can come in now."

"Wait a minute, how did you do this? And why didn't you say anything?" Jim asked.

"I'm sorry, but some plans work best when the least amount of people know about it," Alan advised. "If you must know, I wasn't bird watching. I was getting the security code for the alarm system and I lifted the manager's keys when she set them down about 10 minutes before closing."

"Aha! Not bad Alan." Jim slapped him on the shoulder. He was just glad he didn't have to do it. A million consequences would go through his head before he made a decision. It would probably end with them sleeping outside; open to attacks from people inebriated with lawless intent. Thankfully, Alan's generation was cut from a different cloth and that was a plus in this situation.

CHAPTER TWELVE

They sat in contorted positions against the wall and used each other's shoulders as pillows while they slept. Arguably, Ian had the best seat. He lay across Azalea's lap while Ilia slept in Carol's arms. A chime echoed from the clock in the hallway. Azalea yawned and stretched. Her back and bottom ached from sitting on the hard floor.

"That was the most uncomfortable night's rest I've ever had." Jim's voice was raspy. His face scrunched up when he yawned. He was mentally exhausted and wanted to be back at the ranch where he had control over his surroundings.

They gathered their belongings and left the castle. Alan trailed behind them, twirling the keys on his index finger. He separated himself from the group, went around the castle, and tossed the keys into the lower bailey. As far as he was concerned, they'd done no harm.

"Alan." Azalea looked around for her husband.
Jim scratched his head, "He was just here. There he is."
Alan jogged to Azalea. They walked to the entrance of the park to the van. Jim was surprised to see an open path, he wasted no time getting in the van, and everyone followed his lead.

Alan turned toward Jim, "So, what's the plan?"

"I'm going to the police station." One day of babysitting was all he could take. He had to take care of himself and his wife. After all, he taught for 40 years in the Poughkeepsie school district.

"They should be with their families."

"Are you and your wife coming?" Carol asked.

"Sure, why not," he replied.

Jim drove to the nearest police station. They entered with the children. "How can I help you?" An officer at the front desk asked.

Jim gave the officer the details of the previous day. She took his statement and gave him the police report number. He was glad this part of the ordeal was over. All he wanted to do was get out of New York City.

"So, can I go now?" Jim asked the officer.

"Yes, we have all your information and the name of the girl, except for the boy. You only have his first name?"

"That's right. He was sitting beside his mother on the sidewalk when we found him. She didn't have any identification on her. She was robbed by a homeless man."

Ilia sat on the bench holding the toddler. "Okay kids, it was nice knowing you. I hope everything works out," Jim said and walked to the exit.

Carol hugged the children. "Be good, okay?" She walked to the exit.

"Excuse me Sir, you can't leave them here," the officer said.

Jim turned around abruptly. "Why not? They're not my kids." His voice went up to a baritone.

"I'm aware of that, but with communications down, we are unable to contact Children Services. We are reserving the squad cars for emergencies only. So it's best the children stay with you."

Jim shook his head.

"But I don't live in the city. I'm going back to Poughkeepsie when I leave here."

His cheeks reddened, he clenched his lips and mumbled to Carol under his breath, *"What kind of malarkey is this? I could be a serial killer or a pedophile. I can't believe they expect us to take them home."*

"Don't make a scene. Let's go," Carol said as they walked out the door.

Alan and Azalea stood outside the front door.

"Did everything go okay?" Alan asked.

"I don't want to talk about it! We're leaving this mad house." Jim walked past Alan and Azalea. The first few minutes of the drive was as tense as a crane lifting a heavy load. Jim exhaled and his shoulders lowered. "That didn't go well. I expected a different result." No one said a word and continued to look ahead or out the window.

"I'm sorry for snapping at you Alan. I'm tired. I want to go home."

"I understand, apology accepted." Alan had other things to worry about at this point.

"The officer said we have to keep the children until the families come looking for them," Carol explained.

Alan nodded his head. "I'm sure it will all work out for the best." "It was nice hanging out with you guys, but Azalea and I will be getting off on the corner of 79th street. We're staying at my sister's place." He hadn't called Lynn. She would be wondering where they were. "We'll be in town for a few days. Then we're out of here."

"I'll leave you with our contact information just in case you need anything." Jim said to Alan. Azalea smiled at Carol as she took the sheet of paper. "Sure, why not."

The Polanski's could have been resting comfortably at home since yesterday, but Azalea wanted to make sure the couple weren't taking advantage of the attacks to abduct children. It was clear the Borland's had the children's best interest at heart. It was time for them to go home. The van arrived at the corner of 79th street and the couple got out of the car.

"Thank you for allowing us to tag along with you," Alan said.

"You're welcome. Take care." They waved and walked away.

Jim turned on the radio as he drove away.

"'You're listening to Hot 97. New York, this is your boy Luke, with the latest news. The Rikers Island

prison has been attacked. We contacted them for comment and they released the following statement: *Regrettably, the North Infirmary and Taylor House, which houses adolescents and males, have been compromised. We are working diligently to keep the situation under control. In addition, we have requested assistance from the police department to contain the situation. Citizens should stay indoors and as always, report anything suspicious.*

This is crazy. Let's hope the boys in blue handle their business. Coming up after the commercial break is "Don't Play, by Tonya Stevens. HOT 97 FM."'

They drove to the Holland tunnel. "Well at least we're out of the city. I'm surprised we were able to make it this far," Carol huffed.

"True." Jim yawned.

The van coursed through the tunnel as traffic tightened at the end. A loud rumble followed by what sounded like a fleet of trucks unloading bricks simultaneously ensued.

"What's that?" Jim felt pressure in his eardrum.
Carol looked back, and froze in place.

"What is it Carol?"
The van jolted, sending his head forward, colliding with the steering wheel.

"Jim—," she shouted as she held Ian. The van filled with blood-curdling screams as the Hudson River gushed through the tunnel, pushing the van forward. They managed to stay afloat, but water gushed through the seams. The force of the water sent them crashing forward into other cars, sandwiching them at the end of the tunnel. The water receded, but the entrance to the tunnel in New York was flooded.

The red folds of his droopy eyelids hung beyond his eye, but way above his elongated ears and wet nose. The dogs' sad lips hung almost as long as his ears and drool dripped from the corners of its mouth. A warm slimy sensation traveled upside his left cheek. She brushed the dog away.

"Cut that out Duke." Duke's owner shouted from the open window in the back of the truck.

His eyes opened and closed for a few minutes then opened. Jim quickly prompted himself up on his elbow.

"AHH, What the hell—"

"It's okay. I'm here," Carol said to calm him.

"UGH, his breath smells like fish and shit. I'm sick to my stomach." The hound dog continued to look at Jim and occasionally blinked.

"What's going on?" He sat up. "My head hurts."

"You were knocked out when the impact sent us crashing forward. This young man was nice enough to come to our rescue."

Jim looked over his shoulder at the man and tipped his hat.

"His name is Brian."

Jim straightened his back against the lining of the truck.

"I see that the kids are ok."

"Thank goodness," Carol said.

Brian turned unto a dirt road and dropped them off at their ranch in Poughkeepsie. Jim's head was pounding, but he tried not to think about it. He was happy to be home. He shook Brian's hand.

"Thank you for getting us out of the tunnel safely." He drove away; a cloud of dust encased them as the truck accelerated.

CHAPTER THIRTEEN

A bomb went off at the uptown jail on the other side of Manhattan. Inmates poured on the streets of New York City like rats. Moments later, various hospitals throughout the boroughs were bombed. Corpses from the previous day's attack lay slain in the streets. Flies hovered around bloated bodies ripened by the intense heat. Charred human remains gave off the putrid aromatic mixture of pork, liver, and leather tanned over a flame.

Fear gripped the city, and the streets of NY were relatively clear except for law enforcement, the FBI, National Guard troops, and escapees. Widespread looting broke out as the situation continued to spiral out of control. Many barricaded themselves inside their homes and apartments to keep criminals out. Crimes occurred everyday, but with the prisoners on the loose, being a victim was almost a certainty. It was a great motivator for the citizens to batten down. National Guard troops shot escapees who refused to yield and the streets were littered with shell casings. They piled bodies into the back of their Humvee's and transported them to the makeshift morgue for identification.

Alan and Azalea arrived at his sister's apartment. He knocked on the door, but no one responded. Inside, Lynn sat on a recliner watching the news. Against the inside of the front door sat a mahogany chest. Alan continued to knock on the door.

"Lynn, it's me, Alan." Lynn walked to the door and looked through the peephole, pushed the chest aside and let them in.

"Are you okay? Why didn't you call? I was worried."

"We're fine. What's the news saying about what's going on?" Alan asked.

"A lot."

Alan picked up the remote control and turned up the volume. In a long list of escapees, another zoo animal had escaped. It joined the group consisting of a cow, baboon, pig, ram, Egyptian cobra, and a peacock that escaped the zoo walls. The captivating lure of the city was irresistible. Buildings became trees, noise likened to nature's animal calls, and streets became green pastures. This time a tiger escaped and mauled a few criminals and an innocent bystander before it was captured. When bombs were going off in the city, a tiger was the least of their concern. All he cared about was finding out what was going on. He changed the channel. Live footage of the chaotic scene downtown was on display for all to see. Alan stood there taking in all the information. He had witnessed the bombings the day before, but seeing it on TV was a different story. Alan wondered how he would keep them safe outside these walls.

"Can you help me with this?" Lynn walked over to the door. Alan helped her move the chest.

"I know it looks bad but everything will be back to normal in a few days," Lynn said. "I'm going to lie down. I'm exhausted."

Eventually, people ventured out in the city. All the while, attacks were still occurring on a daily basis. The pantry was low on food so Lynn offered to go out shopping. Alan knew it was too dangerous. He offered to go instead.

"I can't let you go out there without me. I'm coming too," Azalea said.

"All right then."

Alan locked the door behind them. Alan and his wife made their way outside. An officer stopped and asked them where they were going as they walked down the block.

"You shouldn't be out here. It's dangerous. There's a lot of criminals on the loose."

"But, we're going to the store for food," Azalea said.

"It's too dangerous."

Alan held his wife by the hand, and led her back into the building. When you need food to survive, some things become secondary. Alan knew it was dangerous, but he was the man of the house. He had to hunt for food for his family.

"What are we going to do?"

"Don't worry. I know what I'm doing."

"I think he's gone," Alan said.

They cautiously pressed their backs against the building. They both emerged and walked to the supermarket. Alan and his wife sidestepped bodies that lined the streets. The farther down the street they went, the state of businesses deteriorated. The glass entrance of the grocery store was shattered, and the shelves were empty except for condiments and cleaning supplies, so they tried another location. The results were the same. They walked to the apartment empty handed. When they arrived at the brownstone, the front door's glass laid in ruin. Alan stepped through the door and held Azalea's hand as she stepped in. He ran up the hallway to Lynn's apartment. Lynn's door hung on one hinge. He entered cautiously.

"Oh my." Alan held the side of his forehead.

"Lynn, are you okay?" No one responded. He entered and traveled through the living room with his wife close behind. Alan looked around the room. It did not look good. Alan hoped whoever did this was long gone and his sister was safe. "My Goodness, Alan look." Azalea pointed to the bloodstains on the wall.

"Lynn." he walked throughout the ransacked apartment. His heart rate increased with each step.

He bent over, and placed his hand on his knees.

"It's not safe here, we have to go."

They walked to the lobby and left the building. Alan stopped outside the front door and looked down the street.

"It's clear. Let's go."

Alan and Azalea watched in disbelief. A street sweeper plowed through the street, pushing bodies out into the middle of the road. Remnants of dried blood remained where the bodies were left to wither away. The smell from the makeshift morgues a few blocks away traveled up the block. Alan covered his nose. They walked past a group of soldiers patrolling the area. Unclaimed bodies, which accounted for more than half of the dead, were cremated there. Rats the size of cats congregated on the sidewalk like gangs eating whatever they desired. Some even dared to approach people. A good '*YAH*' usually got them to run. Clearly, an invisible beast had devoured a chunk of New York City.

The further Northwest they went, on the corner of Central Park West and 79th street, the number of people increased. Alan kept Azalea close, just in case some psycho decided to test his punk meter. He'd probably fail, but he'd die trying.

"What's going on?" They mingled into the crowd. Someone in the crowd said, "I think someone is going to open the museum."

Alan and Azalea eased their way out of the crowd.

Azalea rubbed her stomach. "What are we going to do?"

Alan looked at his wife. "A hotel would be great." He spent the next hour calling hotels in Manhattan. In the end, he realized that the only ones with vacancies were the posh hotels with a price above his pay grade. The affordable hotels were filled. "I think we should stick around. The hotels we can afford are booked."

A locksmith emerged from the crowd and offered to open the museum. He used his tools to open the door. The large glass windows on the museum were dusty, but otherwise untouched by survivors thus far. The doors opened. The crowd entered the museum in an orderly fashion and branched off to various exhibits. On a normal day, it would look like a guided tour. After everyone entered, the locksmith locked and chained the doors.

It was impossible to make a conscious effort to make sense out of the horrible things that occurred the past few days. He gravitated to his favorite part of the museum, the Egyptian exhibit. Azalea stopped as they got near the sarcophagus.

"Are you okay?" He saw the hairs on her hands stand up.

"I don't know. It's like an overwhelming electrical energy pulling me to the sarcophagus."

"Let's go over there by the sphinx," Alan suggested. Azalea bent over, gripped her stomach, and grimaced. Alan held her firmly. "Are you okay?" She began to take deep breaths and closed her eyes.

"Have a seat." He moved her to the Egyptian stool. She sat down and continued to pace her breathing.

"We're not supposed to touch the exhibits," Azalea said.

Alan scoffed. "I don't think they care." Alan had to put things in perspective.

In an unusual mix of strangers, one never knew what to expect. In here, it's every man for themselves. Whether they liked it or not, everyone was on their own. Some volunteered to be runners. They gathered food and brought it to the museum. The food would then be stored in shopping carts in the middle of the art gallery for anyone to take at leisure. Everything ran smoothly at first, but some people started to take more than they could eat. With food decreasing, attitudes changed.

"I think we should find someplace else to stay, Alan. The air is getting thick in here."

In the distance, they heard voices getting louder. "I swear, if you don't give me my wallet I'm going to fuck you up," a man said. He held another man's shirt in the grip of his fist. "A picture of my wife and daughter are in there. It's all I have left to remind me of them."

"I don't have your wallet. Money can't buy shit anyway. Food is the currency of the realm," the accused said.

A woman parted her way through the crowd that formed around the two men.

"Is this yours? I found it by a bag of clothes next to a blanket."

He looked at it. "Yes." He loosened his grip on the man, grabbed the wallet, and opened it. The accused stumbled to the floor. The man walked out of the room, pushing people out of the way.

"What an asshole," someone said.

Alan and his wife distanced themselves from the group and moved to a less populated area of the museum.

Azalea stood near the hallway that led to one of the nature exhibits. Warm liquid gushed through her undergarments pooling on the tiles below her. She tugged on Alan's shirt. "I need to get to the hospital."

Alan ran to the museum door, held the handle and shook it.

"Let me out of here! I need to go and get help!"

"Calm down." The locksmith came over. The keys dangled from his carpenter pants.

"My wife's in labor."

The locksmith opened the door. Alan ran up the block to the National Guard hub.

"My wife's in labor. I need help," he panted his words in-between breaths.

A guardsman stood at the entrance of the tent.

"I will have to get permission. I'll be right back."

The officer returned with two other men. They drove Alan back to the museum. The brawny officers brought in a gurney and Azalea eased her way unto it.

"Everything is going to be okay," Alan said and kissed her hand.

They rode to Mt. Sinai Hospital, entered through the emergency room doors and bypassed the registration desk. The nurses' station was deserted. A woman emerged from behind a drawn curtain, dressed in civilian clothing.

"Can I help you gentlemen?"

"We have a woman who's in labor," the guardsman said.

"I'm the only one here, besides a patient who developed gangrene from his injuries."

"Can we bring the patient in?"

"No one's here. All of the doctors, nurses and patients are stationed at New York Presbyterian Hospital. You'll have to take her there. They allowed me to stay here with my boy. He has gangrene in over 80 percent of his body. There was nothing else they could do but provide medication to ease his suffering."

"I'm sorry to hear that. I'll keep you in my prayers," the guardsman said before leaving.

They returned to the Humvee and traveled to New York Presbyterian Hospital.
A contraction came on. Azalea's fingernails went deep into her husband's flesh.

"It's okay, just breathe." All right then, let's go."

"Please give me something for the pain," Azalea said to the nurse when they arrived at the hospital.

"I'm sorry, but we've been out of meds for the past few days. We have been unable to restock because the bridges are closed. You'll have to go natural on this one." The nurse checked her vitals. Alan paced back and forth in the room.

"Would you stop, you're making me nervous."

"I'm Sorry." He walked over and held her hands. "You've been in labor for eight hours. How long is this going to take?"

"Excuse me; I'm the one having my *Oh-La-La* stretched to the hilt." She let go of his hand.

"I'm sorry. I'm anxious to see the baby." He knelt at her bed. She stared at him without saying a word.

"Ahh, Eh, Eh, woo, Eh, Eh, woo." She paced her breathing. "Oh please. Ahh, ahh hmmm, hmmm." Azalea tried her best not to scream.

The nurse entered the room and examined her to determine how many centimeters she had dilated.

"It looks like you're ready. We'll take you to the delivery room." The nurse transferred her to a larger bed and transported her to the delivery room.

"Alan."

"I'm right here." Alan walked behind her. He took a deep breath, and said, "I can do this."

The baby's head extended out and moved underneath the pelvic bone. "When you feel the next contraction, I want you to push as hard as you can."

"Okay, Push."

"Um mm, emmmmhh," Azalea mumbled.

"You're doing great." Alan wiped the sweat from her forehead.

"Push," the nurse said.

"Ahh—." Azalea's body trembled as she pushed.

"There you go." The doctor said. He removed the umbilical cord from around the baby's neck as it inched out of the birth canal. The doctor held the baby.

"Would you like to cut the cord?" The doctor gave Alan the scissors. He took a deep breath, took the scissors from the doctor and cut the umbilical cord. The nurse wiped the mucus off with a warm cloth, took a blood sample from the heel and took a footprint for the chart.

"Is the baby okay? I can't hear him," Azalea raised her head off the pillow.

"Congratulations, you have a baby girl." The nurse wrapped the baby in a blanket and placed her in Alan's arms. He walked over to his wife's side.

Azalea's eye filled with tears. He put the baby on her chest.

"She's beautiful." She kissed her.

Azalea gave Alan the baby.

"I'm having another contraction." Alan gave the nurse the baby.

"The placenta is coming out. Push and you'll be done," the nurse said.

"Okay, its out." The nurse called the doctor over. He examined the extra tissue that came out with the placenta. "Give her a shot of Syntocin."

"Mr. Polanski, can I speak with you a moment." They entered the hallway. "Your wife has placental abruption. This occurs when the uterine lining separates from the uterus. She's losing a lot of blood, but we are giving her something to control the bleeding. It's a miracle that both of them made it this far. We'll keep them for observation for two days."

"Thank you." He shook the doctor's hand.

Alan sat on the side of the bed. "She has a full head of hair." He ran his fingers through her Auburn curls as she lay in the bassinet. He kissed Azalea on the forehead.

"Thank you for giving me a beautiful daughter."

"You're welcome."

He twirled a strand of his wife's strawberry-blond hair around his index finger. She smiled, displaying the gap between her front teeth.

"When we get out of here, I want a real meal. One that doesn't taste like seasoned cardboard."

"It will be the first thing we do. After that, we can find a way to get back to Yellow Springs."

The nurse entered the room. "How are you feeling?"

"I'm fine, just a little weak."

The nurse checked her vitals and wheeled the baby back to the nursery.

"I'm going to try to get some shuteye." He kissed her on the lips.

"Goodnight."

He leaned back in the recliner and covered himself with a blanket.

Alan could feel the warmth of the sun through the windows even with the AC on. He opened his eyes, yawned, and stretched. Alan had his first decent night's rest since the attacks. He got up and went to the bathroom.

"Today's the day." Alan looked at his reflection in the mirror. He left the bathroom, and walked over to the bed. His eyes followed a large bloodstain on the side of the sheet that led to a puddle on the floor.

"Azalea." He jerked her arm. "Azalea, are you okay?" Alan tilted her body and lifted the sheet that was saturated with blood. He looked at her. Azalea's head lay sideways and her eyes were closed.

"Azalea." He shook her, lifting her slightly. The nurse walked in, "Oh my." She pressed the emergency button and took Azalea's vitals. "I'll be right back." The doctor entered the room. "We have a low BP. I'm sorry sir, but you'll have to leave the room." Alan walked backward out of the room. The pulse monitor line gradually fell and then flat-lined. "Charge the Automated External Defibrillator."

"Ready." The nurse said, as the doctor placed the plates on Azaleas chest. The current pulled her body up and then it fell back like a sack of coal.

"Again!"

The monitor briefly displayed a small elevation and then returned to a straight line. The doctor glanced at his watch.

"Time of death, 9:35AM." He turned off the switch on the monitor, and then walked into the waiting room. Alan stood up when he entered. "How is she?"

"I'm sorry sir, but your wife didn't make it." Alan brushed by the doctor and ran down the hall. He held her and wept. Alan laid her back down on the bed gently and sat beside it. Tears flowed from his eyes. The nurse entered.

"I'm sorry for your loss." Alan continued to stare at the wall. "Mr. Polanski, I know you're in a lot of pain, but your daughter is doing well and she'll be discharged. You have to be strong for her. She needs you."

"I can't do this without her," Alan finally spoke, but he was distant.

"You'll be fine." she patted him on the shoulder, left the room and returned with the baby. The nurse took out a bag filled with formula, a blanket and a pack of diapers from underneath the bassinet.

"This should last you two weeks."

"I appreciate your help." He extended his hand and she shook it. He wrapped his daughter in a blanket and left the room.

CHAPTER FOURTEEN

Alan walked through the corridor. Each step he took, felt like the floor liquefied beneath him. The end of the hall seemed further away the more he walked. Patients occupied the corridor in wheel chairs and beds. Alan looked down at his daughter. Her existence was the only thing that felt real.

"Alan, is that you?"

He stopped, looked to the left and right, then continued to walk.

"Alan."

He looked behind him.

"Is that—?" His eyes couldn't focus. "We thought we lost you." Lynn sat in a wheelchair with her forehead and forearm bandaged.

"You almost did, but an officer intervened in the nick of time," Lynn said. "Is this the new addition to our family?"

"Yes." Alan's word held no enthusiasm. She knew that he was looking forward to being a dad. If she did not know any better, she would think he was coming down from a high but it was not her brother's modus operandi.

He looked down the hall.

"What's wrong?"

"Azalea. She's dead."

Lynn embraced Alan and rubbed his back.

"I'm so sorry. We'll get through this. I promise."

"I was just about to leave. Are you coming?" Alan said.

"My injuries are minor. Let's go."

They waited at the bus stop outside the hospital for hours. Buses came, but they were filled. After awhile they decided to walk. He figured it was better to get somewhere slowly instead of nowhere fast.

"All right, this is as far as I can go," Lynn stopped and leaned against a building.

Somewhere along the way, a few military hummers passed. One of them stopped, which happened to be the same group of officers that took him and his wife to the hospital the day before. "Where are you off to?" asked one of them.

"I want to go home, but I'm not sure it's possible now, so could you take us back to the museum?"

The museum seemed stranger than before. Peculiar looks caused the sweat on his saturated back to chill his spine. The walls around him felt like they were shrinking by the second. Alan doubled back to evade the crowd and went into another exhibit area he hadn't seen before. The Bodies Exhibit sign hung from the ceiling. Lynn followed close behind him, weaving through strangers that occupied the museum. She grew uneasy by the second. The dry musty air left little to be desired.

"Even with the door off its hinge," Lynn looked around the room; her apartment was homier than this psych ward. "Great! An exhibit of dead people."
Lynn looked around the room and swayed her shoulder-length blonde dread locks. Alan glanced at her and lowered his eyes. Her words had breached a delicate matter.

"I'm sorry. It was an inappropriate thing to say."

It was bad enough that he had the death of his wife to mull over, now he was faced with a collage of dead cadavers with life-like eyes staring at him. The faint smell of dried meat permeated the room. Bodies displayed in what would be the norm if they were living, left an eerie impression. In front of him was a cadaver of a pregnant woman laying on her side with a portion of the tissue of her stomach cut away, displaying an unborn fetus inside. To the left, another body cut down the center. On the right, a woman posed on a swing with her legs ajar and her organs were exposed. Alan's body began to tremble. Cold sweat traveled across his forehead. He leaned up against the wall and looked down at his daughter.

"I can't stay here." Alan walked out of the exhibit and Lynn followed. They left the museum and walked up the block to the National Guard hub. The officer who helped him before sat on a step nearby, eating a sandwich. Alan approached him.

"I need one more favor."

The guardsman took a bite of the sandwich. "What do you need?" He took another bite.

"Can you take us to the Port Authority Bus terminal on 42nd street? I need to get out of the city."

"You sure you want to do that? It's crazy down there. The other day we were stationed outside with M16's. Next thing you know, fights broke out because somebody didn't want to wait their turn. Ultimately, it turned into a full-blown riot. This is the wrong time to be pissing people off. We had to use pepper spray to cool them off. You have a baby on your hands, which will make it more dangerous. But if you want to go, I'll take you," the guardsman said.

"I'll take my chances."

When they arrived at the Port Authority bus terminal, Alan was relieved to be one step closer to leaving, but sad that he'd be leaving a piece of himself behind. To utter or mention her name was painful. Death was permanent— there was no coming back from that. A man was ahead of them in line. He looked ahead and saw there were two Customer Service Representatives. One called the customer ahead of them and the other sat there peering at nothing in particular. Time seemed to drag while they waited for assistance along the other passengers. Alan's patience waned as he stared into the abyss of busy travelers hustling to their gate.

"Excuse me. Can you help me?" The customer service representative shrugged his shoulders and rotated his eyes.

"Yeah, I can do that."

Alan walked up to the counter and purchased their tickets. The representative printed their tickets and circled the gate numbers. Alan walked away and shook his head, "Some people have no business working with the public."

The departure time came and went without a boarding call. Eventually, ticket holders were tired of looking at their watches and reverted to staring at one another. It was nothing surprising; they were rarely on time for afternoon departures. A woman paced in the waiting area while busy having a philosophical conversation with herself. Alan glanced at the clock on the wall, two hours late and counting. He walked off his frustration as disillusioned customers waited in limbo. Lynn sat with the baby and waited but moved frequently to relieve the discomfort from the metal weaved chairs.

Angry passengers yelled at the representative in close range, wielding the wrath of unattended oral hygiene. They were tired of answering the same question, 'when will the bus be here?' They have abandoned ship for extended periods. Angry customers loomed like sharks as the representatives resurfaced. A passenger rehashed her day's events of being put on the wrong bus. Now she was stranded in New York with no bus available for her destination until 9 AM the following day. The representative was tired of apologizing for her circumstance. He moved on to the next customer. She's not alone in her circumstance. The look on their weary faces filled with morning drool dried on the corner of their mouths and red eyes told the story.

Alan lost the love of his life, and now he had to raise their baby alone. The other passenger's complaints seemed absurd compared to his loss.

Finally, the bus arrived and everyone lined up for departure. Alan was glad the re-hasher was not on his bus route. He had a feeling she'd tell her story for miles. Alan was happy to leave the chaos behind. Most of the passengers knew that their connections would be gone by the time they arrive at the transfer point, and it was almost certain that when they arrived at their destination, things would be as they left them. Unfortunately, Alan's life would never be the same. He had always liked driving across the country, but leaving without Azalea was too much to bear.

The intercom announced that the bus would begin loading. The passengers lined up at the gate. It was their turn to board. The tickets were checked, bags tagged, and they were allowed to board. Alan stepped up into the colossal bus, crossed his fingers, and visually scanned for a vacant seat up front. Maybe he would hit the jackpot and have two seats all to himself. If he was that lucky, he could sit with Lynn. They could take turns caring for the baby and have a marginal night's rest. Although, sleeping might not be possible, due to the hum of the tires gripping the asphalt and the constant hiss as the bus cuts through the wind.

The criterion of the scan was also for cranky babies and senior citizens. It didn't feel right to think that way, but after what they had been through, a bit of peace wouldn't be so bad. He recalled on the trip to New York he sat next to an older man who talked about World War II for six hours. Alan tried to ignore him, but it didn't work. Then, he resorted to pretending to be asleep. It urged the man to ask him if he was awake. The stories ended when the man fell asleep. On a trip to Kentucky, a baby kept crying even though he ate. Alan came to the following conclusion; babies and senior citizens can be equally whiney.

Alan found a seat up front. Lynn wasn't so lucky. She sat next to a woman whose eyes looked like someone scared her, but it was *Crazy Eyes*. Alan was glad he did not have to sit in the back. He felt bad for Lynn and the other passengers in the back of the bus. If passengers were brave enough to use the restroom, by the time they arrived in Pennsylvania, a lingering scent of urine or a number two would travel down the aisle. As far as Alan was concerned, the only thing he planned on smelling was his wife's favorite scarf he had tucked in his jacket. He put it under his nose and inhaled, taking in the aroma of Elizabeth Taylors' White Diamonds perfume; a tear streamed down his cheek. He laid his head on the back of the seat and wiped the corner of his eyes.

Their bus made a few short stops in Mount Laurel NJ, and Philadelphia PA, before it arrived at the Pittsburgh PA bus station where they had a one-hour layover.
The driver turned on the light and made an announcement: "Everyone must leave the bus for refueling." They stood in line, exited the bus, and went into the waiting area. Lynn threw a blanket over her to shield the baby from the moist air. The passengers exited single file into the chilly 2 AM air. Alan and Lynn entered the building; the bright lights strained their pupils from the sudden adjustment. Everyone looked tired here. Some were waiting at the gate in line for boarding. Others sat on the metal chairs. Alan sat and calculated how many more hours they had to endure.

In the meantime, the kids of other passengers were entertaining themselves. A toddler ran past him, did the Tom Cruise Risky Business dance, and topped it with a split. At the end of the waiting area, a man stood with a small child and a teenage girl wearing a shirtdress. Everyone seemed to be looking at her briefly before looking away. An Amish couple on the opposite side of them shielded the eyes of their children.

From Alan's vantage point, he could not see anything until she walked toward the restrooms. When she turned around, he noticed the dress fit like a shirt. Half of her buttocks were showing and it was clear she had no underwear on or wore a G-string. The dress failed to accommodate her hourglass hips and boisterous bottom. She wasn't bothered by the lack of clothing nor did she fear indecent exposure charges.

Alan felt sick to his stomach. Women looked at the teen in disbelief, whispering to other passengers. The men didn't seem to care. She walked back and forth as if she were at a fashion week event at Bryant Park. Then out of nowhere, she approached Lynn.

"What time is the bus leaving?" Lynn gave her the stink eye.

"I don't know. Sorry."

The girl walked away, mooning Lynn and everyone else as she sashayed out the door. He was appalled by her brazen behavior, and he felt like gouging his eyes out.

The time had come to board again for the final part of the trip to Yellow Springs. Alan regained his seat and mentally checked off a list: no crying babies, no World War II stories, and the absence of stench. The driver turned the lights off and Alan managed to drift into a light sleep. The deeper he went into the REM stages, the image of a glob of blood and mucus harvesting a blood-sucking fetus. It ripped and clawed its way through its host. The fetus' eyes opened and nostrils flexed. The first breath smothered the mother. Alan jerked forward and his eyes opened. He felt his heart vibrating against his rib cage. He looked to his left and saw a woman who was probably in her sixties. She scooted over to Alan and whispered, "You smell that little poop? That was me." Alan was shocked by the unladylike actions of the woman and scooted to the end of his seat, and covered his nose hoping to escape the volatile wind. For the rest of the trip, he stayed awake fearing the farting bandit would release another stink bomb.

Two hours behind schedule, the Dawdling bus arrived at Yellow Springs, Ohio bus station. Alan was tired.

The morning crust that accumulated on his face flaked when he yawned. He couldn't begin to imagine what he was going to tell Azalea's parents. He retrieved his carry-on bag from the overhead compartment and sat down. He looked back at Lynn. She rolled her eyes and exhaled. Alan felt bad for her. He could only imagine what she endured in the back of the bus.

The bus driver made the final announcement.

"Good morning, passengers. We will be pulling into the Bus Terminal shortly. Please take all of your belongings with you if this is your destination. If you are transferring, there will be information on the display boards inside the terminal. On behalf of the Dawdling Bus Lines, I'd like to thank you for riding with us and we hope to take you to future destinations."

For the next three weeks, Jim and Carol took care of Ilia and Ian. Though saddened from their ordeal, the children found comfort among the fields and animals on the couple's ranch. Then the Borland's received a phone call.

"Carol. The police found their families. Children Services will be out to retrieve them tomorrow." He tried to hide his excitement. The last thing he wanted to do was to upset his wife.

"That's wonderful!" she was excited, but her body grew tense.

"What's the matter, dear?" He put his arm around her.

"I'll miss them." He turned and hugged her.

"They'll be fine. I promise." He consoled Carol. Later in the evening, they sat with Ilia and explained to her that she would be going home the following day. She was excited to see her family again but she would miss the Borland's. Her grandparents died before she was born and the Borland's' were a great substitute.

The next day, Children Services arrived and pulled up in the yard. A man and woman got out.

"Steven Smith, Children Services." Mr. Smith extended his hand and Jim shook it. Carol stood beside him. The woman smiled and remained silent.

"I'm here to pick up Ilia Walters." He read from a sheet of paper.

"What about Ian?" The couple asked, as Jim sneaked a peek at Mr. Smith's paperwork.

"No one has come forward to claim guardianship."
Jim looked up and resumed eye contact with the man. This can't be happening again.
When the agency called, they said they were picking up Ilia. I didn't listen carefully.

"We'll continue to look for his family," Mr. Smith said. Finding his parents is a priority; Jim was glad it was their job and not his.

"So what happens now?"

"Under normal circumstances, we'd take the child into custody and put him into foster care. However, with the current state of things in New York City, it's not possible. If the officers who took your police report had kept the children until we picked them up, we would have been able to place him. With all that has happened, and the other kids who were orphaned when their parents died in the attack, we were bombarded. We don't have any foster parents to place him with." Mr. Smith cleared his throat.

"I took the liberty to do a background check on you and your wife and we see no reason why you can't be his foster parent until we find his next of kin. We would provide monetary assistance. Is that something you would be willing to do?"

"We're not interested in the money. We want him to be safe." Jim looked at his wife. He knew how close his wife had grown to the boy and how hard it would be for her to let them go.

Ian rested his head on Carol's shoulder. She kissed him and he gurgled and smiled.

"All right then, we'll take care of him," Carol said. Jim moved closer to his wife and held her hand. "We will." Ilia stood next to the Borland's trying not to cry. It was a bittersweet moment. She missed her family.

"Ilia, you'll be going with Mr. Smith." Sniffles erupted, and silent tears flowed down Ilia's face. Carol tried to hold back the tears but they trickle down her cheeks.

"I can't do this Jim." She hugged Ilia. "I love you. Take care of yourself." Carol gave Ian to Jim and went back inside the house. The woman with Mr. Smith put Ilia in the car and then got in. Jim walked behind them as the car slowly drove down the dirt road. Ilia knelt on the back seat, to get one last glimpse of the Borland's. She looked out the window; it was a long farewell to her temporary home. Jim stopped when the car increased speed and turned on the asphalt road. Ian rested his head on Jim's shoulder and waved.

CHAPTER FIFTEEN

Ian thought he'd heard all of Jim's stories before. It was the first time he heard *this* story. He was amazed at how much his father remembered. Jim looked toward the window.

"It's not so bad here. You get used to it after a while."

Ian looked at him. "I enjoyed our visit. I'll come see you soon." Jim turned and looked at Ian. His forehead bunched. "Are you the new orderly?"

Ian felt a lump rise in his throat. "No. I'm your son, Ian."

Jim looked at him. "Oh that's right. When did you get here?"

"Actually I've been here awhile. I was about to leave." Ian kissed him on the forehead. "I'll see you soon."

The conductor came through the aisle of each car to collect tickets. Ian took his ticket out of his backpack and gave it to the conductor. He tore off the ticket and gave Ian the summary stub. The train slowly pulled out of the station and quickly picked up speed. Ian peered through the window, taking in the view of upstate New York as the train left the station. The hour and forty-five-minute ride on the Metro-North Railroad to New York City was like a moving painting of a comparison of country and city life.

He was relieved to leave Poughkeepsie. It was a mental chore going through the emotional difficulties of seeing his father. The thought of Jim living in a care facility was heartbreaking but it was out of his control. Seeing Anya again might change his mood. She would understand his pain. They have lived with loss.

Anya waited at Grand Central Station. *Ian will be here soon.* She looked forward to hanging out with him. She spotted him from a distance when the doors opened and passengers entered the platform. Ian's jet-black hair, mild tan skin and piercing pale blue eyes, made him easy to spot in the crowd of passengers. Anya put her hand in the air and waved to get his attention. He saw her and walked over.

"Hi. How are you doing?" He stopped in front of Anya.

"I'm fine. What about you?"

Ian exhaled, "Not too good. My dad's condition is getting worse."

Anya saw water welling up in his eyes.

"It will be okay," she patted his back.

Anya suggested they go to the park. They laid on the Great Lawn in Central Park on a blanket feasting on tiny canisters of Chinese food. The lawn was crowded with sunbathers in bikinis. Some lay on towels bra-less on their stomachs basking in the sun.

"I think I'm on to something," Anya chewed the remnants of food and swallowed.

"What did you find out?" Ian looked at her.

"I spoke to Dave, a retired cop who was a detective during the time the attacks occurred. He was a valuable resource. I've been looking into it for weeks now." Anya ate another spoonful of food.

Ian sat with legs folded inside the other. He looked at her funny and took a sip of his drink.

"I've been looking into an organization called the New Life Criterion."

The name sounded familiar to Ian. As a child, he remembered his classmate invited him to a community gathering in the Catskills. Everyone sat at large tables with an abundance of food. So much so, that it seemed like an eternal feast. Every time a platter emptied, it was replaced with another. He never saw that much food on a single table before or since. Anya continued to talk, but Ian's mind was somewhere else. His thoughts drifted back to a time he rarely thought about.

After the bombing, New York City experienced unspeakable hardships and Upstate New Yorkers were not immune. Many of them worked in the city. However, those who had livestock and planted crops fared well. The Borland's were blessed with both. The unemployment rate was at 15 percent. Many were out of work and depended on charity to survive. Soup kitchens were a fixture and were found within a five to 10 miles radius. Lines of people wrapped around the block, waiting to eat food or to pick up food donations. Their faces housed deep-set eyes and cheekbones so visible it seemed to carve into the flesh. Hope seemed like a fallacy when their bellies were empty and their children emaciated.

New Life Criterion stood out from other organizations. They spoke to the heart of their troubles by feeding, clothing and providing shelter to the homeless in their communities' dormitories.

"Ian." Anya waved her hand in front of his eyes.

"I heard you. I was thinking about something. He rubbed his index finger and thumb over the frame of his chin. "I know of them."

"Do you have any other leads?"

"A few, but for now I'm looking into New Life." Anya looked at Ian; he did not seem pleased.

"I don't think they're capable of doing something that terrible."

"How would you know?" Anya asked and she sat up.

"I'm unofficially apart of the organization." His face soured.

Anya sat there looking at him for a moment without saying anything.

"A friend invited me when I was 10 years old, and I continued to go until I moved to Yellow Springs a year ago to stay with my dad's younger sister, and her husband."

"I see." Anya didn't know what else to say.

"Trust me, there's no way. I spent many weekends planting crops with other youth members. When the crops matured, we harvested them. The elders cooked and we served the food to the needy in the Community Dinner Hall." He paused for a moment. "They provided life coaches." He counted on his fingers. "Job training for the unemployed, and job placement."

"Okay." Anya hoped to quell the defense mode he trickled into. It was clear his involvement and pre-conceived notions would hinder her investigation.

"It's not them." Keep looking. Ian said nothing for a few minutes.

"That was the best chicken fried rice I've ever had." She looked at Ian then up at the skyline where the trees ended and the skyscrapers took over.

"I agree." Ian's response lacked enthusiasm. He swirled his utensil around inside the empty carton. His thoughts were in motion. He wondered if there was any substance to Anya's claim.

CHAPTER SIXTEEN

Sundays brought on a low-tide feeling that made Lynn feel like staying indoors and relaxing. She'd had a long day, week, and had an even longer summer ahead with many deadlines, and she felt overwhelmed. Anya made her life easier. She kept the apartment in order, and on a few occasions, cooked when she felt the urge. Lynn decided to cook a special dinner to show Anya her appreciation.

Lynn sat at the dinner table waiting for her to come home. She heard keys jingling and the lock turned. Anya walked down the hallway.

"Good evening auntie." She entered the dining room. Her eyes widened when she saw the table.

"What's the occasion?" You can feed at least four people with all this food."

"You're probably right." Lynn stood up.

"Ian would have a field day with all this food," Anya said.

"You can invite him if you like."

"I'll give him a call and see what he says."

Ian walked Anya home from the train station to her apartment building, and then walked back to the subway station. He was about to swipe his metro card when his cell phone rang. He answered and listened.

"I'll be there in 10 minutes." He left the subway station. It wasn't even a block away. He arrived in half the time he estimated.

The three of them sat at the dining table eating and sharing light conversation when the doorbell rang.

"Anya, can you get that please?" Lynn asked.

"Sure." Anya got up and walked to the front door.

She looked through the peephole, and then opened the door. It was Todd, holding a Yorkie with a red ribbon tied on a strand of its hair. She opened the door and the hallway erupted with squeals of excitement. Anya did not give Todd a chance to say anything. She took the dog from his hands. Ian walked down the hall to see what was going on. Lynn followed behind him. When they arrived at the end of the hallway, Anya walked towards them and Todd followed behind her. Lynn smiled when she saw Anya holding the Yorkie like a baby.

"I didn't know you had a dog. It is so cute," Anya stroked the dog's hair.

"Actually, it's not his dog. I thought you would like to have one." Lynn said.

Anya pranced up and down and hugged her aunt.

"Thank you."

"Come on. Let's get back to the food before it gets cold. Would you like to join us, Todd?" Lynn asked as they walked back to the dining room.

"Nah, I'm not hungry."

"I insist; after all, I couldn't surprise Anya without you."

"Okay, I'll stay."

Ian stood on the sidelines with his hands in his pockets.

"Hi." Todd walked past Ian.

"Hey," Todd said under his breath.

"The dining room is this way." Lynn walked into the dining room. They all sat at the table. Lynn and Anya sat on the end and Ian and Todd sat in the middle, facing each other. Todd sat there slicing his beef while giving Ian a death stare, as if he was dueling for his share of grub. After a while, Ian avoided eye contact by engaging in conversation with Anya.

"Anya, can I talk to you in private?" Todd asked.

He turned to Lynn. "May I be excused?"

"Sure, go ahead."

"Thank you." Todd got up and left the dining room. Anya followed him. He stood in the hallway fidgeting.

"I want to apologize for how I behaved at prom. I was a jerk. I'm sorry for upsetting you and for hurting Leslie. I—." He stopped for a moment and ran his hands through his hair.

"I like you. It's frustrating when you care about someone and you're invisible to them. It hurts." Todd's eyes filled with tears, yet he didn't allow any to fall.

Anya stood there, listening to Todd pour his heart out. She exhaled and extended both of her hands and he placed his in hers.

"I'm sorry. It wasn't intentional." She held his hands firmly.

Ian leaned back in his chair. Anya released Todd's hands and hugged him. He saw Todd smell her hair. He straightened his chair.

"Is everything okay?" Lynn asked.

"Yes." Ian played with his food.

Todd and Anya came back to the dining room.

"I'll be leaving now." Todd said.

"Thanks for dropping the puppy off. I couldn't have pulled this off without you." Lynn got up from the table, walked over and kissed Todd on the cheek.

"Good night." Lynn walked with Todd to the front door and he left.

She returned to the dining room, took a sip of her wine and glanced at Ian, then at Anya. Lynn could sense negative energy fuming from Ian, while Anya sat there as if everything was hunky-dory.

"How's dinner?" Lynn asked her eyes traveled from Ian to Anya.

"Delicious. Thanks for inviting me, but I think I should go; it's getting late."

Anya got up and walked with him to the front door.

"Good night." Ian opened the door and walked into the hallway.

"See you later," Anya said. Ian walked down the hallway and left the building. She sighed and walked back to the dining room. Anya picked up the Yorkie. It licked her on the chin and she squirmed.

"Eww."

Lynn cleared her throat.

"They're both fond of you. Whether you like it or not, you're going to have to choose." Lynn cleared the table.

"We're just friends." Anya tried to convince Lynn.

"If that's what you want to believe." Anya got up from the table and took the dishes to the kitchen. Then she got the other platters of food and covered them. She rolled her sleeves up and started clearing the scraps from their plates in the garbage disposal.

"I'll take care of it. You've been a great helper and a joy to have around." Lynn hugged Anya and kissed her on the forehead.

"Thank you. Are you sure you don't want me to help?"

"I'm sure." Lynn drank the remnants of the wine.

Anya went into the living room and took the puppy out of the kennel box Lynn had brought out when she wasn't looking.

"What's your name? You look like a Paige to me." The puppy licked the side of her cheek.

"Paige it is then."

She walked into her bedroom, laid on her bed, and held Paige on her tummy and fell asleep.

Anya sat on her bed and looked through the window. The worst part of summer in the city was the rainstorms. Umbrellas were useless, and raincoats were mere decoration when the sky over the city decided to release the water works. Poor Paige hadn't been taken out for a walk in days because it hadn't stopped raining. Beads of rain hit the window and streaked to the bottom. The house phone rang and she answered.

"Hello."

"Hi, stranger."

"What's going on with you? You haven't called me."

"Sorry Dad, I've been busy. There is so much to do and see here."

"Is that all you've been doing?"

"What do you mean?"

"I found your composition book. You've been looking into the attacks on New York. All these months you've been lying to me."

"No dad. You've been lying to me for 16 years." Anya elevated her voice.

"Don't raise your voice at me young lady," He said sternly. "I'm coming to get you on Wednesday."

"But Dad—."

"You're coming home."

Anya held the phone away from her face for a moment and screamed. She startled Paige and Paige barked at her.

"Bye, Dad." Anya hung up.

"Come on Paige we have work to do." Anya attached the leash to Paige's collar.

Alan was not about to let his daughter go off on some vigilante operation on her own. Anya hanging up on him only fueled the fire. He was even more determined to get her back home. He called her back. She stared at the phone. Anya did not intend to answer his call. She grabbed an umbrella and Paige and left the apartment.

Rain came down in sheets, causing her umbrella to bend under the pressure. Anya ran down the sidewalk holding Paige. She took shelter in a pizza parlor a block away. Anya waited under the awning for the rain to subside. *Maybe this wasn't such a good idea after all.* She entered the pizzeria, ordered two slices of pizza and a drink. Anya sat with Paige in her lap at the booth in the corner and ate her slice. She tore the other slice into small squares and fed it to Paige.

"What are we going to do?" Anya moved her face closer to Paige's face.

Anya waited until the rain subsided; she walked home. When she got inside the apartment, the light on the answering machine was blinking. It was all or nothing; she had nothing to lose. She pressed the 'retrieve message' button and listened to the messages her father left. She'd probably be grounded for the next three years, but it was worth the trouble. Anya deleted his messages. She went into the kitchen, and stuffed food items in a backpack. Anya went to her bedroom and added a few clothes.

"Come on Paige, we're going on a field trip." She sat at the edge of her bed and dressed Paige in a dog sweater and Cubic Zirconium collar.

"You look fabulous, yes you do," she said. Paige growled and scratched at the sweater. Anya put the backpack over her shoulder, scooped Paige off the bed and left the apartment.

She called Ian as she walked down the sidewalk, hoping he would pick up. The phone rang for the maximum rings, it seemed. She was about to hang up when Ian picked up.

"It's me. Where are you?"

"I'm at Grand Central Station. Then I'll catch the Metro North to Poughkeepsie."

"So soon? You didn't mention you were leaving so soon when I saw you the other day."

"What do you care? You've got Todd to keep your company."

"Hey that's not fair. I didn't think it mattered to you," she said.

"Look, I have to go." Ian hung up the phone.

"Crap." Anya turned off the cell phone. She calmed herself by taking deep breaths.

"Think! Think!" she said to herself. Anya decided to take the subway to Grand Central Station. When she got there, she paced the ticket area, contemplating all the things that could go wrong and the possibility of eliminating a suspect from her investigation, before her dad cut the wind out of her sail. She flexed her limbs and walked up to the ticket counter.

"A round trip ticket to Poughkeepsie please," she said to the ticket agent behind the Plexiglas.

During the ride to Poughkeepsie, Anya brainstormed about the reasons why anyone would try to take down a major city. *Whomever did this must have gained something by destroying the city? She patted Paige's head. I should have listened to Ian.* Silent tears ran down her cheek. She wiped the tears away with the back of her hand.

"Hmm." *Maybe the positive contributions made by the organization were a sign they were not responsible.* She questioned herself. She had to get up close and find out for herself. Anya glanced at her watch. It read 9 PM.

Lynn would be home soon. When she realized Anya was not there, things would run amuck. When Anya arrived at the Poughkeepsie station it was dark, and her fear heightened. All the planning went down the drain when she threw caution to the wind and acted out of desperation. She had no idea what to do or where to go from here, because she left her notes at home, but she managed to remember the address.

Paige looked happy and carefree while Anya was nervous. She stepped off the train on the dark platform and walked toward the exit. The roads were dark, except for a streetlight that flickered a few feet away. She walked toward the city bus stop but stopped short of the bench and stayed close to the Metro North station. Anya didn't want to be snatched up by a stranger. There was a man sitting, waiting for the bus. A few minutes later, the bus pulled up and she walked over. The dim street light cast a faint shadow on the street. The man stood up and stood aside.

"Ladies first."

Her heart was beating so fast, she didn't hear him. She entered the bus, paid her fare and sat in the front row. The man walked up the steps. A hoodie shielded the side of his face from her. After he paid his fare, he removed the hoodie and walked past her to the back of the bus. She immediately recognized him as he walked behind the yellow line.

"Ian."

"What are you doing here?" He kept walking and sat in the back of the bus.

Anya got up, walked to the back, and sat beside him.

"My dad is coming to get me. I wasn't supposed to leave until next week." Ian put his headphones on and turned on the IPod in his pocket.

"Ian," she shouted, and removed his headphone.

"I want you to take me to New Life Criterion, please."

Ian stared at her. "Do you know what time it is? Don't answer that question, I'll do the honors. It is past your bedtime. I thought we went over this already."

"Please Ian. I just want to check it out."

Ian's blood was boiling and he'd had enough of her so-called investigation. He looked at her and saw how determined she was. How could he be selfish and deny her what *could* lead to her peace of mind.

"Fine. If you want to check it out, I will take you; but you're wrong about them."

"We'll have to transfer to another bus. We're going to need transfers." Ian walked up to the driver and asked for two transfers. The bus driver gave him a small speech. "You are supposed to get the transfers when you pay your fare."

"Sorry about that. We changed our plans."

The driver continued to grumble, but he gave Ian the transfers.

Ian walked back to his seat shaking his head.

An hour later, they arrive at New Life Criterion. The front of the building was well lit and the front parking lot empty.

"See, no one's here," Ian said when the bus stopped.

"I've come too far to go back now. Let's look around the back." They got off the bus and walked around the back of the building. At least twelve vehicles were parked in the lot.

"See. Let's go in," Anya said.

They entered through an unlocked back door and walked through a storage room that housed the food pantry, chairs, and tables. They walked down the hall into the main lobby. It was empty, and Ian went in the opposite direction. "Let's check the main hall," he said.

They entered the main hall and noticed the podium and chairs were empty. Anya looked around the room. Plaques with the words affirmation, hope, love, faith, and charity written on them decorated the walls. They continued to explore the building, and left the main hall and went down a staircase to a lower level. At the end of the staircase was a series of doors on each side and a double-door in the center. Ultraviolet lights in the ceiling flickered when Anya walked down the corridor with Ian beside her.

CHAPTER SEVENTEEN

Lynn arrived home. She poured a glass of wine, turned on the television, and sat on the sofa. Before long, she fell asleep. A few hours later, she woke up to the sound of a loud beep. The channel went offline. She got up, turned off the TV, and walked past Anya's room. She backtracked and looked into the room. The room was empty. She looked at her watch, 2 AM.

"Anya! Paige!" she shouted as she walked throughout the apartment.

When there was no reply. She realized the unthinkable. Her hand trembled as she picked up the phone.

"9-1-1. What's your emergency?"

"My niece. She's missing."

Alan received the call parent's dread. His daughter was missing. He booked the next flight out of Dayton International Airport to John F. Kennedy Airport.

Lynn searched for a recent picture of her niece to give to the police. The same picture that was on the front-page of the Yellow Springs Newspaper was used to circulate the news circuit.

Ian and Anya stood outside the double doors in the hallway. They heard voices coming from inside. Anya jumped to look through the tiny window in the upper part of the door, but she was too short. Ian saw a group of men seated in three rows and one man standing, addressing the group. It was Tillman Ellis the leader of the organization.

"My brothers, we are the harbingers of the revelations to come. We are at the crossroad of our era. The world is broken. Humanity is broken. We must purge the land, filter the weeds, and plant new seeds. The time is upon us to cleanse the earth of the pestilence and perverse nature of humanity.

We are the fallen angels, sent to rise against his once favored servants. It will be a temporary hell, but it is necessary to bring heaven on earth. Rise up and carry out the will of our father."

"Are you willing to make the necessary sacrifices?" Tillman asked.

"We will carry out the will of our father," the men replied collectively.

Ian's facial expression changed from annoyed to terrified. He looked at Anya and whispered, "We need to get out of here."

"I agree. Let's go." Anya turned around, and the zipper on her backpack scratched against the double doors.

"Shit—." Anya looked at Ian and they both ran toward the staircase. A group of men pushed through the door and ran behind them down the hall.

"Hey! What are you doing here?" one man said.
Anya and Ian ran to the base of the stairs. Another man grabbed Anya's backpack. Paige and Anya fell to the floor. Paige ran away whining. Ian, who was a step ahead of her, stopped in his tracks once he realized what happened, and turned around. He walked toward them.

"Why are you snooping around?" Tillman asked. He gripped Anya's biceps. She grimaced.

"You're hurting me."

"Please don't hurt her," Ian begged. He moved in closer and the other man held his hands behind his back.

Tillman pointed to Ian.

"Aren't you the kid from the Community Food Center?" he asked.

"Yes." Ian trembled.

"Lock them in the utility closet," Tillman ordered. They pushed them inside the dark closet and closed the door. Ian reached for the light; brooms and mops tumbled around them. He found it and flicked the switch.

"I told you this was a bad idea." Ian kicked the mop bucket. A sour smell filled the closet when brown water spilled on the floor.

Anya rolled her eyes. "Oh great. Gross water."

"Shh, they're talking," Ian said. They listened to the men talking at the end of the hallway.

"We're going to have to put our plans into motion sooner than expected," Tillman said. "They heard what we said. We can't let them go. It could jeopardize our plans. For every cause, sacrifices are made."

"We will do the will of our father," the men said.

"But the boy is one of us," one of the men said.

"He's not a member. Only our father's children have a place in his kingdom," Tillman shouted.

The look on their faces spoke volumes. Ian tried to remain calm, but Anya saw the tension building on his face. He kept passing his hands over his hair. She was relieved when he put his hands in his pocket. The men stopped talking. The closet door opened. Two men stood there, one of them had rope in his hands.

The police tip line was flooded with calls concerning Anya's disappearance, but few leads panned out. There was surveillance footage of her getting on the subway. The ticket agent at Metro-North recognized Anya and called the hotline. Dave, the retired cop got wind of her disappearance and chimed in. He gave an interview to a local news station.

"I think the kid is looking for something, but I'm not sure what that is. She seemed like a good kid."

"Do you think she ran away from home?" The reporter held the microphone below Dave's mouth.

"I have no clue. You'll have to ask her parents." Dave kept it simple. He was purposely vague to reporters, but behind the scenes, he had given detectives information about Anya's interest in the attack.

"I think the kid is tracking down the people responsible for the August third attacks."
Once the police heard that, they were alarmed. Anya's whereabouts after she got off Metro-North was unknown. NYPD notified the Poughkeepsie police department to help them further.

Alan arrived in New York. He felt like his world was coming apart once again like it did so long ago. Only this time instead of losing his wife, his daughter was missing. It was the first time he'd been back to New York. He promised long ago to never return. All the emotions he felt back then came rushing back.

CHAPTER EIGHTEEN

Alan felt his world crumbling around him with Anya missing. He caught a cab to the police station to meet Lynn. She was in the waiting room when he arrived. She walked over to him and they embraced.

"I'm so sorry."

"It's not your fault. Actually, I think I'm the one who started this whole ordeal."

"What do you mean?"

"I called yesterday. I told her I would be picking her up today."

"For what? She's scheduled to leave next week."

"I left a message for you yesterday on the answering machine."

She looked at him as if he was crazy. "There was no message on the machine." Then she thought for a moment.

"That little bugger," she shook her head.

"It's okay Lynn, it doesn't matter now. I just want my daughter home safe."

An officer walked over to Lynn.

"Is this her father?"

"Yes." Alan shook the officer's hand.

"I'm Officer Henderson. We have some new leads on your daughter's whereabouts. A bus dropped them off at a building in the Catskills. We have a team on the way there."

Anya and Ian sat in the back of a van with their hands tied, back to back and mouths gagged. In various crates around them, were explosives attached to timing devices. The engine started, and they drove away from the New Life Criterion building. Anya closed her eyes and thought of her mother. If this was her last day on earth, at least her mother would be waiting in heaven for her with open arms. Her eyes began to water. Anya's hands ached, but she was able to move her fingers. It would be all her fault if anything happened to him.

Ian felt defeated. Everything he believed in was an illusion. He couldn't decide what was worse, leading them to their demise or being an unwilling accomplice to a band of 'Mad Maxes' who wanted to hurt the only girl he cared about. By the time the whole ordeal was over, it probably wouldn't matter. He wouldn't be alive to proclaim his innocence. Their heads began to nod and they both fell asleep.

The police arrived at New Life Criterion and surrounded the building. A swat team entered and searched the building, "All clear, they're not here." The swat team left the building while the officers searched the common areas for any evidence.

"I think we have something," one of the officers said. He held up a map with markers on it. He gave the map to the lead detective.

"Where did you get this?" the detective asked.

"The basement office," the officer responded.

He looked over the marked map and called the sergeant, "We need the FBI on this ASAP." The case was bigger than they thought.

At the station, Alan sat with Lynn holding her hands. He closed his eyes and said a silent prayer. *Dear lord, please let my daughter be okay.*

Lynn walked to the counter.

"Are there any new developments?" she asked the officer behind the desk.

"No, Ma'am, we haven't heard anything. Officer Henderson will fill you in when he gets an update from the officers on site."

They were in the back of the van for a long time before the car finally stopped. They were tucked away from the world and the people who loved them.

This must be the worse way to die, Ian thought. *But then again everyone who thinks they are going to die thinks that way unless they go peacefully in their sleep.* On the Anya couldn't decide what was worse, waiting or starving. The day's seemed to blend. Yet, she estimated at least two days had passed since they were taken.

One thing that was clear to them both was the area was unusually quiet, except for the sound of distant cars and low flying planes. Anya wasn't sure how long they could survive without food or water, but she knew their bodies were beginning to feed on itself. She kept going in and out of consciousness and saw things that weren't there. She heard drumming and the sound of her classmates dancing to music at the prom.

"I want the major roadways blocked off, no one goes through without being searched," the lead FBI investigator said. He stood next to Catskill Police Chief Raymond as he spoke to his colleagues before dispatching them to various locations.

"No slip up's. We can't afford any casualties," Chief Raymond said before ending the meeting.

"Alright, let's get these people behind bars before they can do any harm."

Alan embodied the definition of helplessness while he waited for word about his daughter's whereabouts. A million things ran through his head, and nothing could make him feel less responsible for her vigilante approach to arrive at the truth. He could have saved himself the heartache if he had told her the truth. Lynn watched Alan as he made his rounds. He paced back and forth in the waiting room. After a few hours of watching, Alan pace, Officer Henderson approached him.

"Mr. Polanski, it might be best if you go home and relax a bit. We will call you as soon as we get any news. Staying here is not going to make things move any quicker. In fact, it will make it seem like an eternity."

Alan flared his nostrils with each breath and glared at the officer.

"Do you have a kid?"

"Tell you what; if your kid goes missing, see if you can relax." Alan advanced closer to the officer.

The officer's right hand slowly came to rest on the gun holster. Lynn rushed to Alan's side.

"He's just trying to help."

The officer exhaled and walked away, shaking his head. Alan reluctantly left the station. Lynn followed him outside and they drove home.

It would be days before Todd found out about what happened to Anya. He tried to reach Lynn, but her phone line was busy. Todd went over to her place but no one was home. By the third day, he'd had enough, and went down to the closest police station to her apartment.

When he walked into the station, he spotted Alan at the counter.

"Mr. Polanski."

Alan turned around. "Hi Todd."

"I heard about what happened to Anya. I came down to help in any way I can."

"I appreciate the gesture, but I'm not sure if there is anything you can do."

"We can go looking for her."

"Okay Todd. We all want her back home safe, but getting overly anxious is not going to help." At that moment, Alan realized that Officer Henderson was right. He felt bad.

The town of Yellow Springs was distraught. A local daughter was lost in the Big Apple. The community organized several prayer vigils. Crowds of natives from neighboring counties and visitors gathered with candles at night to pray for her safe return. The Polanski's lawn became a shrine of teddy bears, balloons, poster boards with personal messages from classmates, and flowers. Anya and Ian was the number one topic in town.

Brittany felt like the most important part of her was lost without Anya. To make matters worse, she had no idea how to get in touch with her aunt in New York. Anya promised she'd call her during the summer, but she never called. Brittany didn't think anything at first, but when she heard about Anya's abduction on the evening news a few days ago, her heart sank. Brittany spent the next few days combing through old albums of pictures they took as kids. She couldn't imagine her life without Anya. Brittany promised herself if her friend survived, she'd change her life for the better.

"You know the statistics. The first three hours of an abduction is crucial to the victim's survival. We have to find these kids, and fast." Detective Henderson walked down the hall and went into his Sgt. Lynch's office.

"What are we missing? Did we ever get the results back on the vehicles registered to the organization?"
Sgt. Lynch was on the phone. He paused for a moment, and put his hand over the mouthpiece.

"One second," he said to Detective Henderson. "I'm going to have to call you back. Can I get your number?" he said to the person on the phone, jotted the number down on a piece of paper and hung up.

"I'm going to look into that and get right back to you." Sgt. Lynch walked down the hall to another office. He emerged a few minutes later with a paper in hand.

"We got 'em. Here's the license plate number of a van registered to the group."

Sgt. Lynch called Catskill Police Chief Raymond and they issued an All-Points Bulletin on the vehicle.

Law enforcement got numerous reports of sightings leading up to the Pittsburgh PA area. The Pittsburgh Police Department and NY State Police cordoned off a section of roads to set up roadblocks. The kidnapping had become a multi-state effort, with credible sources of information streaming into the police.

Anya and Ian were in the back of the humid van, drenched in perspiration. Ian's shirt clung to his back. Though physically exhausted, he found the strength to fight with the ropes around his wrists to free himself. The rope loosened and Ian was able to free his hands and untie his feet. He removed the gag from his mouth before falling into a slump. He felt the van moving, and slowly, cooler air entered through the crevice of the door. Anya mumbled as she sat on the uncomfortable rippled floor of the van.

"Shh, I'll get you out." Ian untied her hands, then legs, and finally took the gag from her mouth. The van accelerated to a high speed. *We must be on the highway*, Ian thought. They slowed down to a crawl. Anya looked at Ian. He sensed her fear growing.

"It'll be okay. I won't let anything happen to you."

"Ian, if we don't make it. I'd like you to know—."

"No, were going to make it," he cut her off.

She closed her eyes.

"Okay."

The car came to a complete stop. Anya and Ian saw the flashing blue and red lights through the wire mesh window behind the driver's seat. One lone officer who arrived at the location was in the process of setting up a roadblock when the van drove into the intersection. His fellow officers were en route with the FBI. He pointed his flashlight into the driver's side window.

"Can I see your driver's license and registration please?" the officer said. The driver gave the officer his license and registration. The officer walked back to his car to confirm the driver's information.

"We should go. Now!" the passenger said.

"Nah. Relax. Just act normal and everything will be fine," the driver said.

The officer ran the plates. He walked back to the van to return the documents.

"Thank you." The driver took the paperwork and drove away slowly.

"What happened?"

"I don't know. The police let them go."

"Do something," Anya said. Ian pushed one of the crates over and it crashed to the floor. The officer looked back when he heard the commotion.

He walked back to his cruiser. The computer screen blinked, a match came in for the APB on the plates he had run just a few minutes earlier. He called for backup and gave the location of the last sighting. The officer put on his siren and drove after the van. The driver of the van heard the sirens in the distance, pulled off on a dirt road, and waited until the sirens passed them.

"Damn it. We were so close to catching the bastards," Chief Raymond in Catskill, New York said when he heard the assailants slipped through the roadblock. The FBI and local law enforcement were honing in on suspects in Greene County, and elsewhere. They worried about the well-being of Anya and Ian.

The FBI and police received a call when they arrived at the intersection to help conduct traffic stops. They saw the police car sped down the road. The police cruiser did a hundred-and-eighty-degree turn and sped down the road behind the van. FBI and other police cars followed. Within a matter of five to 10 minutes, the dark highway was lit up with police lights and emergency sirens.

The cruiser whisked by them at least ninety miles-per-hour. It didn't matter that they spotted the van. The driver managed to make evasive moves, turned off the lights and drove on a narrow path that was not readily visible to the police, especially when pursuing a suspect at top speed. They waited in the confines of the trees and shrubs. The van waited there until the air was free of emergency vehicle sirens and drove onto the highway.

After days of waiting, Alan had time to think of all the possible outcomes. He was tired of giving his power over to others who didn't care as much for his daughter as he did. Alan flew out of John F. Kennedy Airport to Pittsburgh. He wasted no time going into the police station and talking with the police. He somehow managed to convince them to allow him to ride along to the scene of the latest sightings.

Alan sat across from the detective's desk.

"Has there been any other sighting?"

"Nothing yet, but don't worry. We'll get the bastards this time," he confided.

"We got a hit. They have been spotted on a stretch of highway and we have cruisers tailing them. It's show time. Let's roll," the detective said. He got up from his desk.
Alan grabbed his jacket and left with the detective.

Lynn stayed in New York. She canceled all of her photo shoots. It would be impossible to concentrate when Anya was missing. Todd had little to do when Lynn canceled her photo shoots. He realized there was nothing he could do, so he went back to Yellow Springs, Ohio. When he arrived, he realized the town was in disarray over Anya's kidnapping. The whole town was praying for Anya. He hoped their prayers would not be ignored.

For the next 150 miles, the van led the police on a chase. The van clipped cars and caused others to crash and run off the road, until finally one of the tires blew out, sending it into a spin, courtesy of the spike strips. The van flipped. The driver went through the windshield, it landed on its side, and the back door flew open. FBI agents surrounded the van. The driver was pinned from the waist down beneath the van. He screamed for help.

"FBI. Come out of the van with your hands up."
One of the agents looked in the passenger side window and saw the passenger slumped to the side. It was clear that his neck was broken by the way the bone pressed against his skin. The agent checked for a pulse. Another agent checked for weapons near the pinned driver.

"All clear."

The lead agent cautiously approached the back of the van. One of the doors lay on the asphalt and the other closed. He saw two people in the back laying across each other. Scattered around them were crates of explosives. He backed away from the van. "Move the perimeter back, we have explosives on deck. We need the bomb squad out here. NOW!"

Their first priority was to get the explosives away from the site and then retrieve the bodies from in and around the van. The bomb squad arrived with their equipment. The police squad cars and FBI vehicles moved to a safe distance. They evaluated the explosives. The devices were not active, but with fuel leaking from the ruptured gas tank it was potentially dangerous. They moved the explosives to another site for detonation. By now, the pinned driver had stopped screaming.

The EMTs moved in to check for survivors. The man pinned in front of the van and the front passengers were dead. They went around to the back of the van with their equipment in hand. A gurney was nearby. He checked both individuals' for a pulse. He signaled the other EMT, "I have a pulse here. We need another gurney." They quickly put the patients on the gurneys and took them to the ambulance.

Alan and Lynn walked down the emergency room hallway looking frantically for Anya's room.

"This one," Lynn walked in the room with Paige in hand. Anya lay on the bed with her head wrapped, connected to all kinds of machines. Alan walked in the room a few seconds later. He broke down when he saw his daughter lying in bed. Alan walked to her and held her hand.

"Hey, Pumpkin," his voice cracked.

Anya's eyes fluttered open.

"I hate it when you call me Pumpkin." Anya squeezed his hand.

"I'm so glad you're okay."

"Hi Auntie. Paige, you're okay. Thank goodness. I was worried about her." Anya said as she looked at Lynn.

"Paige is fine. You kept mumbling to the EMTs that she was in the building. They told the agents and they found her the night we found you. How are you feeling?" Lynn asked. She moved closer to the bed.

"I'm okay." Anya closed her eyes briefly. "Where's Ian?"

"I don't know. We have to go, we got here a little late, and visiting hours is over. We'll be here first thing in the morning." Alan kissed Anya on the forehead and left the room.

"See you tomorrow." Lynn held Anya's hand then loosened her grip as she walked away.

The FBI agent came to take Anya's statement just as she finished her breakfast. They questioned her for over an hour and then left the room. She was happy to get it over with; however, no one answered any of her questions. She turned on the TV and watched the news.

"*Overnight, FBI and NYPD officials apprehended members of the New Life Criterion Organization in connection with the kidnapping of Anya Polanski and Ian Borland. We will provide additional information as it becomes available.*" She muted the television to take a nap.

A patient walked down the hall holding an IV pole. The hospital gown exposed his boxers as he moved through the hall. He stood in the doorway of Anya's room just as she fluffed her pillow and put it under her head. When she saw Ian, her jaw dropped. She cupped her hands over her mouth to muffle her cries. Her hands fell from her mouth. "I thought you were dead."

"You are not getting rid of me that easily." He walked to her bed and sat beside her. Ian ran his hands through her auburn hair.

"How do you feel?" Ian held her hand and took in his surroundings. He was not fond of hospitals but he was grateful they survived. Anya sat up.

"I've never been so happy to see anyone in my entire life." She hugged Ian.

"Same here." He savored her embrace.

"And before you get a chance, you were right about New Life Criterion. I was wrong. Did you hear the news?" Ian asked.

"Yeah, they arrested some people."

"You did it." He held her chin up with his index finger. She smiled and kissed him on the cheek.

"Ahem." Alan cleared his throat and walked in the room.

Anya and Ian separated. Ian stood up. "Hi, Mr. Polanski."

"Hello. Are you okay?"

"I'm fine, thanks for asking," Ian replied.

"Thanks for keeping her safe." Alan shook Ian's hand and patted his shoulder.

"I'll leave you two alone. I'll come back later." Ian left the room. Anya got a glimpse of his underwear when he turned to leave the room. A light chuckle escaped her lips. Alan sat down next to Anya.

"So, is he the one?"

"I think so, dad, but *he* doesn't know it yet." Anya's face beamed as she responded.

"Trust me, he knows. It's okay; you'll always be my girl." Alan hugged his daughter.

A few days before Anya and her father were set to leave New York; she received an unexpected visit from the mayor of New York, Mayor Steven Heinz, accompanied by his bodyguards. Mr. Heinz spoke to Alan and Anya, while Lynn looked on in the living room.

"Your daughter played a major role in dismantling one of the largest cults in the U.S. to date. Tillman Ellis headed the cult. Mr. Ellis forced his followers to turn over all of their savings to New Life Criterion. He bought various properties in upstate New York and created businesses there and in other states. Tillman opened restaurants, laundries, hotels and retail stores. His members worked at his businesses for little or no pay.

Ellis used his profits to stockpile guns, ammunition, and explosives. The organization was huge. They had members in at least 20 other states. They were also responsible for the attacks sixteen years ago."

The mayor's last sentence made everything he said before irrelevant. The depth of the situation stunned Alan. His sixteen-year-old daughter brought down a mighty lion with sheer will power and a pound of rebellion.

"Due to Anya's efforts, we were able to make arrests of over a hundred members, confiscated stockpiles of weapons, and additional arrests are pending. I'm not sure you realize what you have done young lady, but you helped crack a sixteen-year-old cold case. They were planning a major assault across the U.S. and you stopped them."

Alan was filled with so many emotions, but the dominant one was pride. He couldn't even begin to grasp the repercussions of it all.

Mayor Heinz shook Anya's and her father's hands. Anya sat next to her dad, and listened. She was glad she followed her instincts. Alan felt joy and pain all at once. He was happy for Anya but he felt bad that his lies put her in harms' way.

"I don't understand why they would want to kill Americans," Alan said.

"Well, it seems New Life Criterion believed in 'A New Earth.' In their eyes, the only way it could happen was to destroy the world as we know it. Tillman Ellis became obsessed with the second coming of Christ. He managed to convince his followers that he was the new Christ.

But thanks to your daughter, she put a stop to his madness and, for that we would like to present her with a key to the city in a ceremony held on Thursday at City Hall." Alan was overwhelmed. "Anya, I'm so proud of you."

"I would be honored to accept the key to the city on behalf of my mother Azalea Polanski. She was the reason I looked into the attacks."

On the plane ride home, Alan and his daughter had a long conversation about his life with Azalea and all the details of the days following the explosion in New York City. He spoke of her mother's strengths, weaknesses, joys, and pain. It was refreshing to see him open up about everything. It allowed Anya to let go of the ill feelings between them.

Spending the summer in a noisy, adventurous city paled in comparison to coming home to the warmth of a small town with a big personality. The peace one felt in Yellow Springs, Ohio, was beyond value.

The closer she got to her house, the better she felt. Anya peered out of the window of the taxi. Nothing had changed. The cab driver parked in front of the Polanski residence. The driver took out the luggage and put them on the porch. Alan paid the fare and the cab drove away. They sat on the porch and took in the scenery. A collection of trees and flowers adorned the houses on the block. She inhaled the clean air and savored the breeze garnered from the trees.

"I love it here. I wouldn't trade this place for the world," Alan said. Anya looked at him and smiled. "I'll take the luggage inside." Alan got up. "Would you like something to drink?"

"A glass of cold cow."

"One glass of milk coming up," he replied.

Brittany rode up the block, as he returned with Anya's drink. She dropped her bike on the lawn, ran up the steps and hugged Anya. The girls squealed and pranced up and down.

"Hi, Mr. Polanski."

"Hi, Brittany. How's your mom?"

He gave Anya the glass of milk.

"She's doing well. She started going to Alcoholics Anonymous after you left for New York."

"That's great news. And you?"

"I'm doing just fine." She had a glow Anya hadn't seen before.

"I have so much to tell you." Brittany looked excited.

"I'll let you two chat, then. I'll go watch TV or something." He walked into the house; the screen door slammed behind him.

"You look nice," Anya said.

"Thank you. I decided to tone down the raunchy persona. I thought about what you've said and I realized I didn't have to dress that way. I want to thank you for being a positive force in my life."

"Oh Brittany, you're going to make me cry." She hugged her.

"You're the best friend anyone could ask for," Anya said. She patted Britt on the back.

"Anyway," Brittany fluttered her eyelashes. "Todd asked me out when he came back in town."

Anya tried to look happy for her, but deep down she had concerns.

"Good for you. But, be careful. Boys change their minds like they change their socks."

"I promise. I'll keep that in mind." Brittany got up and walked down the steps.

"I have to go. Mom is waiting for me." She got on her bike and rode down the street. Anya came inside and an overwhelming feeling of warmth came over her. She went into the living room and sat next to her father.

"If I could do it all again, I'd be honest with you and tell you everything. I just didn't want you to feel responsible for your mother's death." Anya rested her head on his shoulder. He kissed her on the forehead.

"I'm exhausted. I'm going to bed." Alan went down the hallway to his bedroom.

"Good Night, Dad." Anya got up and went to her room.

She turned on the lamp in the corner of her room and sat in the dim light. Out of the darkness, a light hue of earth tones hovered in the corner by the window. A figure of a faint woman appeared. Her strawberry blond hair glowed and her eyes glistened. She smiled, displaying a gap in her teeth. Anya realized it was her mother. Another blot of color emerged as a baby wrapped in a blanket. Azalea kissed the baby and disappeared.

Anya wrapped her arms around herself, and whispered, "I love you too."

www.ingramcontent.com/pod-product-compliance
Lightning Source LLC
Chambersburg PA
CBHW060624130626
46555CB00002B/647

* 9 7 8 0 9 7 9 4 1 7 2 5 2 *